I0591362

A SUBTLE WAR

A SUBTLE WAR

ENEMY OF MY ENEMY™ BOOK THREE

TIM MARQUITZ   MICHAEL ANDERLE
CRAIG MARTELLE

DISRUPTIVE IMAGINATION®

A Subtle War (this book) is a work of fiction.

All of the characters, organizations, and events portrayed in this novel are either products of the author's imagination or are used fictitiously. Sometimes both.

Copyright © 2018 Tim Marquitz, Michael Anderle and Craig Martelle
Cover by Tom Edwards tomedwardsdesign.com/
Cover copyright © LMBPN Publishing
A Michael Anderle Production

LMBPN Publishing supports the right to free expression and the value of copyright. The purpose of copyright is to encourage writers and artists to produce the creative works that enrich our culture.

The distribution of this book without permission is a theft of the author's intellectual property. If you would like permission to use material from the book (other than for review purposes), please contact support@lmbpn.com. Thank you for your support of the author's rights.

LMBPN Publishing
PMB 196, 2540 South Maryland Pkwy
Las Vegas, NV 89109

First US edition, October 2018

The Kurtherian Gambit (and what happens within / characters / situations / worlds) are copyright © 2015-2018 by Michael T. Anderle and LMBPN Publishing.

A SUBTLE WAR TEAM

Thanks to the JIT Readers

James Caplan
Nicole Emens
Tracey Byrnes
Keith Verret
Peter Manis
Daniel Weigert
Kelly O'Donnell
Micky Cocker

If I've missed anyone, please let me know!

Editor
LKJ Bookmakers

CHAPTER ONE

Taj grinned as the mass of lizard-like Wyyvan soldiers pushed into the dimly-lit room. Their armored footsteps thumped as they stormed forward. The hiss of their heavy breaths as they were filtered through the tubes that moistened the air they breathed seemed to fill the room.

"Let's do this," she called out over the comm to the rest of her crew, who gathered around her.

Without hesitation, Lina, Torbon, and Cabe moved into position, readying to do battle.

Taj triggered her armor, setting it to anti-grav mode, and leapt into the air above the Wyyvans' heads. On instinct, the aliens watched her, raising their weapons to blast her away.

That was when she set off her defense mechanism.

"Flares away!" she shouted to warn her teammates, then twisted in midair as her suit spat out a brilliant array of sparks that erupted all around her, blurring the enemy's vision.

The crew scattered in response, each of their helmet visors automatically adjusting to the sudden burst of light trailing their captain.

"I love you, Dent!" Torbon said into the comm as he circled around the Wyyvan soldiers while admiring the flashy display. He started to fire at the enemy.

"Who doesn't?" Dent answered with the hint of a chuckle in his mechanical voice.

"Probably Cabe," Torbon replied with a grunt as he dove out of the line of Wyyvan fire. "You should give him the crappy armor next time."

"Hey! That's not true," Cabe defended, dropping to his knee and blasting one of the aliens, drawing their wavering eyes his way. "Especially if it means I get gacked on the cool stuff."

"Fear not," Dent answered. "My honor demands I treat you all equally, even if you don't like me as much...*Cabe.*"

"See what you did, Torbon?" Cabe asked. "Now you've got him believing that. I'm so gacked."

"Eyes on the prize, people," Taj called out, dropping through the layer of sparkling flares. "Take out the enemy, then worry about who gets the best gear." She landed in front of a Wyyvan soldier, his eyes going wide behind his visor in surprise, and she latched onto his armored throat.

The soldier went to shoot her, but Taj was already moving. The servos in her suit hummed in her ears as she whipped the alien up and over her shoulder, flinging him hard across the room as if he weighed nothing. He slammed into the wall with a loud *crunch* and slumped to the floor in a heap.

"Besides," Taj went on, "Dent promised *me* all the cool

stuff." She laughed and launched herself back into the air as more of the Wyyvan soldiers spun and started firing in her direction.

"Dent likes me the most," Lina assured, stepping up and letting loose with the automatic blaster rifle the AI had built for her. "I'm the one putting all these things together, remember?"

Bolt after bolt crashed into the mass of alien soldiers. Their armor took the brunt of the blasts, but they staggered back under the onslaught, the attack scattering them and knocking the Wyyvans out of formation.

Torbon dove at the soldiers, dropping low and activating his two energy blades, which jutted from the back of his hands and splayed out to his sides. He darted through the grouping of Wyyvans, weapons trailing, and cut through the legs of four different soldiers.

The Wyyvans shrieked and toppled, clutching at their wounds, and Lina turned her weapon on the still-standing troops, offering cover fire to give Torbon time to get to the other side.

Cabe joined the fight as soon as she stopped her barrage to reload. He circled around the engineer and raised his modified bolt rifle, his favorite weapon. It *boomed* as he pulled the trigger, the sound echoing through the room, and the nearest of the Wyyvans had his head blown off, helmet and all.

"Bloody Rowl!" Cabe howled happily, marching forward.

A smoking crater between his shoulders, the wounded soldier slumped to the ground, and Cabe shot the man beside him in the chest, the wide-eyed alien too busy watching his fellow soldier die to even notice he'd been targeted. He flew backward, trailing black smoke, dead without ever realizing it.

Taj dropped out of the sky again behind two more of the soldiers and set her gun to the side of one's head. A quick tap of the trigger at point blank range sent a bolt tearing through the first's skull, then struck the second in the head. Both dropped with a clatter of armor. Taj spun to face the next foe.

That was when she caught a blast in the gut.

"Ooooof!" she cried out, the blow knocking her back on her butt. Her breath billowed from her lungs as her armor blunted the damage.

The Wyyvan soldier hovered over her, grinning. He took aim at her as she struggled to make her lungs work and shake off the pain and surprise of the unexpected shot that had set her ribs to throbbing. She grunted and went to raise her weapon.

Torbon got to the soldier first.

He skipped past, slicing the Wyyvan's gun barrel in half, sparks flying and leaving tracers on Taj's retinas. His second blade scored a hit on the alien's thigh, driving him to his knee with a pained shout. The useless weapon fell to his side.

"All yours," Torbon laughed as he shot past, going after another soldier whose back was turned to him.

"My pleasure," Taj muttered, her gun up and targeting the wounded alien who'd shot her moments before.

She pulled the trigger and blasted a hole in his stomach. He gasped and clutched his belly, slumping to his side.

"How's it feel, buddy?" she asked, firing again and putting the Wyyvan out of his misery.

"Helps to wait a minute before shooting them if you actually want an answer," Cabe told her over the comm, chuckling.

"It's called a rhetorical question, Cabe," Taj muttered, dusting herself off and climbing back to her feet.

"Then why ask it at all?" he replied.

"Because it makes me feel better," she argued, raising her gun and blasting another of the Wyyvans who'd turned to target her. The alien crumpled to the ground, dead.

That *definitely* made her feel better.

Lina's weapon sounded again, hurling bolt after bolt at the last of the Wyyvans, killing one and driving the other two back on their heels. Torbon cut one down, and Cabe blasted the other, leaving the corpses to topple among the rest of their alien companions, silence overtaking the room in the wake of combat.

Taj walked over, joining the rest of the crew. Adrenaline cooling in her veins, she set a hand to her stomach and grunted. "That's gonna leave a bruise."

"Try not getting shot next time," Torbon told her.

"Always sage advice from this one," Cabe laughed, patting Torbon on his armored shoulder. Torbon's tail flicked back and forth with amusement. *"Just don't get shot,"* Cabe said, mimicking Torbon.

"Easier said than done sometimes," Lina replied, glancing down at a scorch mark on her armor where the last group of enemies had blasted her cleanly in the chest.

"How'd we do, Dent?" Taj asked, ignoring the ache in her belly as the far wall shimmered, cracking open. A squad of custodial bots swarmed out to clean up the mess the crew left behind.

"This training sequence took you several seconds longer than the last," the AI reported. "However, you managed to take out your opponents more efficiently this time around, though you lose points for being struck by one of the android Wyyvans, Taj. The goal is to avoid injury, as Torbon pointed out."

Taj snorted.

Torbon grinned. "Told ya!"

"All in all, though, you're getting better with each attempt," Dent assured. "You're becoming more comfortable with the equipment and the tactics of working together as a group, which is a far cry from the results from when you first started training. It's only taken a few months." Dent chuckled. "That first time was a disaster, let me tell you."

"You don't need to remind us, Dent," Cabe complained. "We were there."

"I have it on video if you'd like to watch it again. Pure comedy," the AI teased. "I've never seen anyone stab themselves before."

"Hey!" Torbon shouted. "In my defense, I tripped over Taj. What the gack was she doing lying on the floor right then?"

"At least it was Lina who killed you, not yourself," Cabe said, grinning so wide his eyeteeth gleamed.

"How was I supposed to know there'd be that much kickback on the gun?" the engineer asked, shaking her head.

"Brrrrrrrrrrrrtttt!" Cabe sounded, falling to his back

comically as he imitated Lina being knocked over by the force of her weapon.

"In her defense," Dent stated, "it *was* the first time any of you managed to kill more than a single opponent with the same attack. She deserves credit for that accolade, at the very least."

"Oh yeah," Torbon chuckled. "Friendly fire massacres are always the best way to earn accolades from combat and if one must begin an attack with a bang, let it be the good guys on the wrong end."

"Would have been worse had anyone survived to whine about it," Lina told him, glaring through her visor at Torbon.

"Hence the reason you continue to train," Dent reassured over the comm. "Always better to fumble and fail in practice than in real life. You can walk away from stun bolts and android opponents programmed not to hurt you seriously. None of your enemies will be so considerate."

"Not that we're ever gonna face any real enemies," Cabe complained. "We've been on-station for six months, and we haven't heard a word from the General or anyone else representing the Etheric Federation since we first got here. It's like they don't want our help."

"They've probably seen our training holos," Lina joked.

"That would definitely explain it," Taj agreed.

She watched as the cleaning crew sped around the room and swept the android carcasses toward the recycling center. They'd been so happy to arrive at *Corzant*, the Federation-aligned space station where the crew had been living ever since they'd been forced to flee Krawlas, their distant home planet, which had been invaded by the lizard-like Wyyvan.

Now, boredom, homesickness, and frustration had settled in—big time.

While Dent had been given access to the station's intelligence databases, and he'd figured out a great way to meld the technology of the Federation and his people, the Dandrinites, the crew had done little more than eat and train the entire time they'd been there.

Not that she was complaining. Things could have been far worse.

She and her people, the Furlorians, originally from Felinus 4, where they'd been made to flee by a previous war, were now safe and sound on *Corzant*. It wasn't the permanent home they'd been promised by General Reynolds, but it was far better than traveling through space in a stolen ship packed to the ceiling with her fellow Furlorians. Being stuffed in anywhere they fit could barely be called surviving.

The General had offered sanctuary for their people and a future home for both the Furlorians and the Dandrinites, whose memory and history lived on inside Dent's mind, only waiting for him to resurrect them.

Taj had been thrilled that day they'd arrived on *Corzant*. But now, with so much time passing and having heard nothing, she was starting to get antsy.

"We gonna do this again?" Cabe asked, interrupting her thoughts, for which she was grateful.

She spent too much time in her head as it was.

Taj shrugged. "Nah," she answered. "I think we're good for today." She glanced at her stomach, running a hand along the armor, which had repaired itself after being shot the last time. She marveled at the suit's resilience for a moment before continuing, "We can probably use a break." Her ribs had started to ache.

"Lunchtime!" Torbon shouted, pumping his arm in the air with excitement.

Cabe grunted and whipped his helmet off, spitting a line of brown nip-juice onto the floor as soon as the helmet was clear. It hit with a splat.

"That's gross," Lina commented as a custodial bot swung over and started cleaning the mess off the ground.

"Are you seriously gumming that stuff while you're wearing your helmet?" Taj asked.

"They don't call it a habit for nothing," he answered, offering a toothy grin.

"You're gonna swallow that stuff one day." Taj shuddered at the thought.

"Wouldn't be the first time," he muttered in response, saying it just loud enough to be heard.

Torbon laughed and shook his head. "Just because the station has provided a gack-ton supply of nip, doesn't mean you need to try and work your way through it all."

"Someone has to," Cabe replied. "Might as well be me. Better than that old Tom, Grady, getting it, right?"

Lina groaned. "Why does it have to be anyone?"

Taj raised a hand to forestall the reply that was obviously ready to spill from Cabe's lips. "Rhetorical question again, so we're clear. Doesn't actually need an answer."

Undeterred by her gesture or comment, Cabe went to reply anyway, but the gentle swish of robes and soft footfalls behind them drew their attention. They spun around to find Eliarar, the spokeswoman of the Ooror people who populated and ran the station.

Tall and wisp-thin, she strode with an elegance that made her appear almost as if she were floating across the floor. Bright white robes trailed behind her like great wings fluttering in the air. Pink eyes met the gazes of the crew, one after another, and she offered each a shallow nod before settling on Taj.

"Training went well?" she asked, her voice ethereal, barely a whisper carried on her soft breath. Though, to her credit, the crew heard and understood her perfectly, likely a testament as to why she remained the representative of her people.

"It could have been worse," Cabe answered, returning her friendly nod.

"It could have been better, too," Torbon argued, not bothering to hide his grin. "A *lot* better."

"Excellent," Eliarar answered, choosing, as she so often did, to ignore Torbon's jokes and replying as if she'd not heard him say anything at all. "The Federation will be pleased to hear of your progress, I'm sure."

Taj looked at the sleek representative, suddenly realizing this was the first time she'd seen the woman in the training arena. In fact, it was the first time she'd seen her anywhere outside of the hangar bay when they'd first arrived or in the administration areas. She'd always summoned the crew to one of the meeting rooms, sending subordinates to hunt them down and bring them along.

"Is something wrong?" Taj asked, finding her presence a bit disconcerting.

Eliarar offered up a gentle smile and shook her head.

"Certainly not," she answered, but before Taj could be relieved by her reply, the woman continued. "However, I've been sent to retrieve you, most expeditiously."

She glanced around as if suspicious, saying nothing for a moment as she waited for the custodial bots to finish up and leave the room, sealing the door behind them. When they were alone, at last, she looked back to the crew.

"General Reynolds wishes to speak with you," she told them, hunkering down and drawing in close as if someone might hear them. "He says it's quite important, so you should hurry."

CHAPTER TWO

"Good to see you all again," General Lance Reynolds told the crew, greeting them as the door closed, leaving them alone in the room, Eliarar having left after saying her goodbyes.

Once more, the General's image hovered on a view screen on the far wall of the room. Unlike the last time they'd seen the human leader, where he'd been excited and happy to see them, the man looked tired, worn out a bit, as if he hadn't had much sleep of late.

"Is everything okay?" Taj asked, moving to the table and taking a seat. The rest of the crew followed her example, slumping into chairs where they could best see the screen.

"Been a hectic few days around here, that's all," he answered, offering up a polite smile that did little to hide his fatigue. "Nothing for you to be concerned about, but thank you."

Taj returned his smile, nodding. She was sure the General wasn't being completely honest with her, but she knew well enough not to ask any more questions regarding his wellbeing. His business was *his* business, and she didn't want to pry.

"What can we do for you, General?" she asked instead, being sure to remind him that they'd offered their services to the Etheric Federation when they'd first come seeking asylum.

The General nodded his appreciation for her getting to the point.

"Well, it looks as if we need your help," he told the crew.

Taj bit back her excitement at hearing those words, and she glanced around the table. Her crew had clearly restrained themselves similarly, but there was nothing to be done about the sly smiles that brightened all their faces.

They were happy to do something besides train day in and day out.

Anything.

"Of course," Taj replied, nodding to the General. "Whatever you need us to do, sir."

"Glad to hear that." General Reynolds grinned. "We've a bit of a situation. Normally, we'd send a ship and crew out to handle it right away, but the location and timing of certain other issues has put us in a bit of a bind. The soonest we can get a ship out there would be a month or more, which might well be too long. We need someone nearby who can do the job for us right away."

Taj straightened in her seat, meeting the General's eyes. Though still a bit sore from being blasted in the ribs, the flush of adrenaline got the best of her. "We're your crew," she answered, thumping a fist on the table.

"You haven't even heard the mission yet," the General said, laughing. "You getting a bit bored out there?"

"And then some," Torbon answered, nodding. "Who do we need to shoot? I'm on it." He went to stand, reaching for his gun, but Taj set a hand on his arm and kept him in his seat.

The General broke into a broad grin at Torbon's enthusiasm. "Well, we're kind of hoping you won't have to shoot anyone. It's not really that kind of mission."

Torbon sighed and slumped deeper into his seat.

"What kind of mission is it then?" Taj asked.

"More of a stealth mission actually," the General answered. "Sneak in, locate the target, and sneak him out. We don't want anyone knowing you were there if we can help it. No fuss, no muss."

"I can do stealthy," Torbon offered.

The rest of the crew turned to stare at him, eyes narrow.

"What?" he asked, raising his hands. "I was born stealthy."

"Says the guy who stabbed himself trying to walk," Cabe retorted.

"Just once," he answered.

"How do you even do that?" Cabe wondered aloud, turning his wrist in an attempt to determine exactly how Torbon had impaled himself on his energy sword.

Taj sighed and glanced back to the General, meeting his wide-eyed stare. "He means in practice, sir," she clarified, knowing they weren't making themselves look good. "Definitely won't happen again. Total fluke."

"He *is* that," Lina mumbled.

"More like a flake," Cabe asserted.

Taj impatiently waved them to silence. "We're ready, General," she said. "We can do this. I give you my word."

"Glad to hear it, Taj," General Reynolds replied, offering her a confident smile. "Your target is similar to yourselves, someone seeking asylum with the Federation. His name is Grom Hadar. He reached out to us with information regarding his government, but then he disappeared as we were arranging his exodus. The last coded message we received from him makes us think he's in danger and that he is in hiding. We're worried about him. We want to get him out of there before something untoward happens to him."

"Understood, sir," Taj told the General. "We'll bring him back safe."

"Excellent. I'll send the details to your AI right now and let you get on your way," he said. "We're counting on you, Taj." He said the last, waved, and shut the connection, the view screen going black.

Taj heard the combined breaths of the crew being let out at once.

"They need us," Torbon crowed, his grin so wide Taj was afraid he'd accidentally swallow his tongue.

"Don't get carried away," Lina warned. "There's no one else close enough to do the job, that's why they want us to do it. We weren't exactly the first names on the list."

"But that's okay," Cabe shot back. "We do this, do it right, get the target home safe and sound, and then next time, next time, our name *is* on the top of the list."

"Let's not pat ourselves on the back just yet," Taj told them. "We don't have any idea where we're going or what we're facing. Save the congratulations until after the mission, yeah?"

Torbon huffed. "You take the fun out of everything," he complained. He turned to Cabe. "I bet she does that even when you two are alone in your quarters, doesn't she?" he asked. *"Don't kiss me yet, you have to meet my gaze romantically first. And don't wrinkle the sheets, I'll just have to make the bed in the morning,"* he said, mimicking Taj's voice, the words spilling out in a squeak.

Cabe's eyes lit up, and he went to laugh, but a steely glare from Taj silenced him before a sound managed to escape. He laid a hand across his mouth to hide the smile he couldn't hold back.

"Don't you dare laugh at that," she threatened, raising a fist and wagging it in his direction. She spun on Torbon, jabbing a finger his way. "And you, the next time you trip over me, you won't have to worry about stabbing yourself..."

"Because she's gonna shoot you," Lina said, cutting in.

"...because I'm gonna shoot you," Taj finished, speaking as if the engineer hadn't said anything.

"If you are finished threatening Torbon's life," Dent interrupted, his mechanical voice coming across the comms, "you might want to make your way to the *Discordant* with all due haste."

"You received the mission details already?" Taj asked.

"I have indeed," he answered, and Taj could almost hear the nod of his non-existent head.

"Well, don't keep us in suspense," Torbon whined.

"Best we do this in private aboard the ship rather than across the comm," Dent told him, brooking no argument.

"The mission, it seems, is quite secretive. We should follow security protocols."

Taj agreed and motioned to the crew to get up and start moving, hearing the determination in the AI's voice. "All right then, everyone, on your feet. No point arguing with Dent."

"Again," Torbon said, shaking his head, "all the fun out of *everything*."

Taj pulled her pistol from its holster and held it up. "That's not true. It'd be all sorts of fun shooting you in the back with stun bolts until we make it back to the ship."

"You wouldn't dare," he growled, standing and puffing his chest out.

Taj made a show out of adjusting the weapon's settings to it lowest and grinned. "Wouldn't I?"

Torbon stood his ground for about three seconds before raising his hands in surrender. "Always so hostile," he muttered, marching from the room.

Taj waited until he was through the door before pulling the trigger. Torbon yipped out in the hallway as a blast caught him in the butt.

"See?" Taj shouted after him. "I'm fun," she said as she pulled the trigger again. "All sorts of fun, huh?"

The only answer was a high-pitched howl from Torbon and the chuckles of Cabe and Lina.

Back aboard the *Discordant*, the small leech craft they'd stolen from the Wyyvan, the crew walked onto the bridge.

"Seriously!" Torbon complained, cradling his tail to his

chest with one arm and holding his butt with his other hand. He winced at every step. "How many times did you need to shoot me?"

"Need?" Taj asked. "It was more a *want* than anything, and I think the ten times more or less satisfied the urge."

"More or less?" Lina asked.

Taj cast a sharpened glare Torbon's direction. "I think that all depends on him. I could squeeze off a few more shots."

"I've learned my lesson, I swear," he muttered, his expression one of utter defeat. "My poor tail," he whined as it twitched in his hand, wisps of smoke curling from its tip.

The door to the bridge hissed shut at their backs once they were inside. Krawg grinned at their arrival, the hulking Ursite hunched over a console near the back. He waved a furry paw arm in their direction.

"Do I need to give you both time-outs?" Dent asked, his voice filtering down from the hidden speakers on the bridge.

"I think we're good now," Taj replied, wandering over and dropping into the captain's chair as the rest of the crew came to stand before her, Krawg joining them a moment later. "How about you clue us in to our mission."

"Straight to the point?" Dent sighed. "Not even a hint of romance, huh?"

"You'd have to ask Cabe about that," Torbon joked, slipping around to hide behind Lina as Taj glared at him.

"Do I need to shoot you again?" Taj asked, drawing her weapon and adjusting the settings higher.

"You might need to shoot *someone*," Dent said, interrupting her tirade.

She put her gun away and looked to the speaker above her head. "Why's that?"

"Well, turns out that General Reynolds is sending you to the planet Zoranthan."

Krawg grunted. "Oooh."

Cabe glanced at the Ursite. "Oooh? What's that supposed to mean?"

Krawg shrugged his furred shoulders. "It means not good."

"Yeah, I got that." Cabe sighed. "I kinda meant *why* is it a bad thing? Care to elaborate?"

"Zoranthan is a feudal world," Dent explained before Krawg could. "Ruled by kings and queens and dukes…"

"Oh my," Lina muttered under her breath.

"While it's not overtly hostile to visitors," Dent continued, "its power structure is in constant flux, the different factions always at war with one another in an effort to claim the biggest piece of the planet. The place can be rather chaotic."

"How's that a bad thing?" Torbon asked. "If everyone's busy trying to steal each other's thrones, they won't even know we're there. We can get in and out before they notice we've even been there. Thanks and good-bye."

"Possibly," Dent answered, but Taj heard a *but* coming. *Sure enough.* "But…it's not the easiest planet to traverse without becoming embroiled in the local struggles, which are everywhere unfortunately. The Federation, according to the data the General supplied, doesn't have more than the barest of footholds there politically."

"Which means?" Taj asked.

"Which means we have a way in, a cover story to get

us onto the planet without overt examination, but that's about it," Dent said. "Once we're there, we're on our own."

"Of course we are," Taj muttered, having expected that seeing how General Reynolds was sending them in to begin with. If there was a real rescue team to be had, he would have sent them instead of the untested Furlorians.

Still, Taj knew this was their chance to prove themselves to the General and the rest of the Federation. No matter what happened, she'd make it work.

"Okay then, when do we leave?"

"There's a ship tasked to take everyone to Zoranthan first thing in the morning," Dent replied.

"A ship?" Lina asked, one eyebrow rising questioningly. "Won't we be taking you...the *Discordant*, I mean?"

"I'll be going," Dent answered, "but the leech ship won't be, unless you feel the urge to explain why a bunch of Furlorians are piloting a stolen Wyyvan spaceship, which just so happens to belong to a mortal enemy of the Zoranthians. Nothing stealthy about arriving like that."

"Good point," Torbon agreed, nodding. "Lizard leech ship bad. Gotcha."

"So then, where will you be?" Lina asked.

The door to the bridge hissed open right then, and the crew spun around as a tall, lithe alien strode into the room.

"I'll be right here," the man answered, the voice clearly Dent's, though it sounded far more natural than it did coming through the speakers, none of the strange mechanical reverb in the sound.

"Holy Rowl!" Cabe exclaimed, blinking as if he couldn't believe what he was seeing.

"Ditto that!" Lina said, clasping onto the edge of Taj's chair. "Is that…"

"A Dandrinite?" the newcomer replied, a gleaming smile spreading across his face. "It most certainly is. The one and only currently in the universe."

"Is that really you, Dent?" Taj asked, kicking herself mentally for asking when the answer was obvious.

"It's me." The newcomer nodded. "Well, sort of. Thanks to the same technology that allowed you to simulate Wyyvans in your training exercises, I was able to cobble together a near-perfect replica of the original form my masters gave me when I was created."

He spun in a tight circle, showing himself off.

"It's got a few rough edges still," he admitted. "I'm not near as handsome as I was originally, but it's otherwise quite similar."

Taj chuckled despite her amazement. Lean but powerful, dressed in a sleek black uniform that accentuated the android's lithe build, she wasn't sure if Dent was joking or not. To her, the body was quite handsome as it was. If there were flaws in it, she certainly couldn't see them.

"Uh," Lina cut in, her eyes narrowing, whiskers pinned back against her cheeks, "aren't you worried about running into the same problem you had before, with the other alien body? Running out of space for all your…uh, you?"

The android Dent shook his head, a finger tapping his temple.

"I'm not *all* in there," his voice answered from the ship's speakers above.

The Dandrinite grinned and waved. Dent's voice coming from the body once more. "What's in here is kind of a shadow image, a copy, just enough to have complete function while my core essence, the *real* me, remains behind in the ship Eliarar and her people have provided. This will allow me to go with you while also remaining in orbit above the planet should we need assistance my android body can't provide."

Lina circled Dent, examining him from every angle, grinning the entire time. "This is…awesome."

"I thought so," Dent answered, matching her grin with one of his own.

"How'd you do this without me?" she asked, straightening and meeting his eyes, her suspicion lurking.

"I recruited some of the training androids," he admitted. "I wanted it to be a surprise."

"It is that," Taj answered, more than impressed by the AI's new form as he came over to join the group gathered by her chair. "I also see you've suited up with one of your armored creations. It looks good on you." She gestured to the slick black uniform he wore, appearing exactly like the ones she and the other crew members had on and had been training in.

"Yes and no," Dent answered.

"Clear as mud as always," Torbon remarked.

"What do you mean?" Taj asked.

"It's different," Lina commented, examining the suit again, running her hand along Dent's back. "Subtly, but definitely different. I can feel it."

"It most certainly is," Dent agreed. "While the suits you are currently wearing shift between powered armor and your day-to-day uniform nicely, this one goes steps beyond that."

"Baby steps or, like, real steps?" Cabe asked.

Dent chuckled. "I guess they could be considered baby steps seeing how I wasn't able to access the full breadth of the Federation's technology—their nanocyte tech is beyond amazing, by the way, not that I managed more than a glance at it before I was locked out—but I've mashed together several concepts into one outfit. Not only will it work as armor as before, and a space suit when completely sealed, it will take on the form of whatever clothes you wish it to with nothing more than a thought."

As he spoke, the drab black, form-fitting uniform transformed before their eyes. Almost as quickly as they realized it was happening, the black shifted to a tuxedo, complete with top hat, white shirt, burgundy tie, and black shoes so shiny they reflected the faces staring at them with awe.

The crew gasped, including Krawg, which sounded more like bellows exhaling.

"Can you change your clothing into anything?" Cabe asked.

Dent nodded. "Anything you can imagine," he answered, and his tuxedo shifted once more, turning into a pair of drab overalls, then to a military uniform—though Taj had no clue what army it represented—and then, at last, to a short, frilly dress with high heels. He curtsied and said, "In case the ladies want a night out, you will be prepared."

"Is it wrong that his legs look great in that getup?" Lina asked, sighing.

"Very wrong," Torbon answered, pretending to hack up

a hairball as he turned away. "So very wrong." His whiskers were pinned to his face, ears twitching.

Dent's dress returned to the plain black uniform, and he grinned at his wide-eyed audience. "The suit will even create accessories such as jewelry and whatnot, but understand that on a molecular level, it's all one piece. While you and everyone else will see the accessory as you imagine it to appear, it can't be removed from the suit and will be reabsorbed into the whole should you or someone else attempt to separate it from the rest. If someone is paying attention when that happens, the whole illusion might well be blown, so be careful with how you choose to accessorize."

"That's amazing," Taj said, admiring Dent's creativity and technical prowess. They'd had none of this type of technology on Krawlas, everything old and worn down and carted over from Felinus 4 by Mama Merr, Beaux, and the rest of the Furlorians when they'd fled.

"The suit also comes with an optic-controller," Dent continued, gesturing to his right eye. "Mine doesn't have it as I already have all the circuits installed in this body, but we will implant one in each of you. This will give you complete access to the suit's systems and link you to me so we can conduct operations privately."

"This is gacking cool and all," Torbon said, "but I'm kinda curious as to why we need such a fancy suit if this is a clandestine mission where we're supposed to keep a low profile."

"About that..." Dent grinned. "I apparently forgot to mention that our cover story is that of visitors from the distant planet of Krawlas," he said, chuckling as he did.

Torbon raised his hands questioningly, glancing around at the crew. "And, other than fuzzy over there…"

Krawg growled.

"…that's exactly what we are."

"Not exactly," Dent told him, pausing a moment before going on. "The Federation has arranged for us to visit Zoranthan as guests of the current ruling family, the Orgesse Clan. They are expecting…uh, royalty."

"Royalty?" Torbon asked.

"That's what I said, wasn't it?" Dent replied, offering up a shrug as a mirror of Torbon's usual response. "We're to pretend we are royalty, or more specifically you four—" He pointed to each of the Furlorians in turn. "—who are to be emissaries of your people, there to enter into a trade agreement with the Orgesse Clan in hopes that you will have something to help them maintain control over the planet. We will be staying at the Orgesse Palace for the duration of our trip."

"Wait!" Taj bristled, sitting up and glaring at the AI's android body. "So, you're saying we're supposed to fly right into the middle of things and pretend to be royalty, all while we try and track down our target and rescue him from Rowl knows where without anyone noticing what we're doing?"

"When you put it like that, it sounds quite preposterous, doesn't it?" Dent answered. "But yes, that's the plan in a nutshell." He grinned. "By the way, how's your acting?"

CHAPTER THREE

Taj drew in a deep breath as she watched the planet of Zoranthan fill the view screen. Brilliant white clouds swam over the blue orb looming before them.

While they'd spent the night preparing and studying everything they could about their target and the planet, seeing it now before them made it glaringly real.

They arrived in the ship the Federation had loaned them, a sleek pleasure ship, the *Arrant*. Dent crowed about it over and over as they activated the gate drives and skipped across the galaxy to Zoranthan.

"This is soooo much better than the *Discordant*," he repeated for the fifteenth time since they'd left port.

Taj ignored him and stared at the view screen, unable to pull her gaze away.

Dozens of ships filled the space around them, each bearing the Orgesse Clan's symbol, a hammer set between a wreath vaguely shaped into a V. Black on red, it stood out sharply against the cold gray steel of the guard ships hovering about to ensure their safe arrival.

"That's an awful lot of firepower hanging around out there," Cabe said, eyes wide and staring as the small armada encircled them.

"The opposition forces, specifically the Talaz and Orv Clans, have aggressive pirate navies," Dent stated.

Taj glanced over her shoulder to watch him speak as she hadn't yet gotten used to his voice coming out of the Dandrinite form.

"After scanning the open Zoranthan databases, both groups are apparently known for raiding incoming visitors in an effort to disrupt Orgesse trade and relations," Dent went on. "It appears to work as a number of distant allies have called off talks after having their envoys assaulted or destroyed while visiting the planet."

"Great," Torbon muttered. "Nothing like getting blasted out of space before our mission even starts."

Den shook his head. "That's unlikely, Torbon," he said. "Scanners are clear, barring the Orgesse crafts and the bot leading us in. It seems the clan is taking every precaution to ensure our arrival is unimpeded, and our sudden arrival has likely forced their political opponents onto their heels."

"The Federation's doing in clearing the way?" Lina asked.

"Unlikely," Dent replied. "If the chatter is to be believed, it's more your supposed royal status that has them up in arms. The prospect of trading them Toradium-42 has the Orgesse Clan excited. It's something they can use to fend off their opponents and gain the upper hand in negotiations. The last thing they want to do is compromise that arrangement or allow their enemies to interfere."

"Did we really need to promise them the Toradium-42?" Torbon asked. His ears fluttered in disgust.

"We're not actually providing it," Taj clarified. "Not that we have access to it to begin with. We're just floating the idea in front of them as cover while we're here. We have the specs on the mineral and can answer questions about it easily enough on the fly, which makes it great leverage and an easy story to run with. Everyone wants a new power source that's gack near inexhaustible. That's what we're offering them...in theory."

"Still feels like we're taking a chance cluing them in to its presence on Krawlas," Torbon countered. "What's to stop them from trying to get the information as to the planet's whereabouts out of us and going there to take it, just like the Wyyvans?"

"He's right. We have no idea what happened to Grom Hadar," Cabe stated. "How do we know the Orgesse Clan isn't responsible for his disappearance?"

Taj shrugged. "We *don't* know, hence the reason General Reynolds sent us here in the first place. It's our job to find out and get Grom out of here before anything happens to him."

"How do we know something hasn't happened to him already?" Torbon wondered aloud, his hands raised. "The General's intel says he disappeared over a week ago, possibly longer."

"We don't know that either," Taj admitted with a sigh, "but if we're walking into this mission thinking the worst from the get-go, we might as well turn around and go back to *Corzant* and forget all about the mission."

"We can't do that," Lina growled.

"Gacking right we can't," Taj agreed. "We're here because there is so little information available regarding what happened to Grom Hadar. It's our job to figure that out and to get him off planet safely. The Federation is depending on us, and I have no intention of letting them, or Grom, down."

Torbon sighed. "Fine."

The *Arrant* shuddered as it docked in a space berth, the guidance bot having led them into place, the ship's systems shutting down in response.

"Game faces on," Taj called out, triggering her suit through the eyepiece, marveling at the seamless integration of the optic.

Within the span of a second, the plain black outfit she wore shifted and changed into her cover outfit. A long, red cloak swooped down her shoulders, its gold embroidery standing out in sharp contrast. Her dress scraped the floor as she turned to admire herself in the reflection from the dark view screen.

Her bangs had been pulled back and tied into a long braid that hung behind her, leaving her face exposed to the world. She sneered at her reflection, annoyed that she had to appear so open, but she couldn't picture royalty hiding behind the fluff of their hair. Her eyes gleamed in the view screen, and she caught the reflection of the others as they willed their suits to transform. She turned to admire them.

The crew looked fantastic.

Cabe and Torbon wore long, grayish-blue coats that

hung to mid-thigh and were accessorized with belts. They wore loose-fitting pants stuffed into calf-high boots that thumped on the floor when they moved.

Lina had split the difference between Taj's and the other's outfits. She had on a long cloak, but she'd eschewed the dress in exchange for a shirt and pants closer to that of Cabe and Torbon, though frillier and in a majestic purple rather than the plain blue-gray the guys chose. She'd also tied her hair back into twin braids that hung nearly to her waist.

Taj glanced past the Furlorians to where Krawg and Dent stood. Dent was expectantly fancy, his outfit what Taj pictured true royalty would wear despite his cover story being that of their emissary and representative.

He wore a sleek silk shirt with a high collar that accentuated his long neck. His pants were tight, form-fitting, and the material shined in the light until the point they disappeared into the tops of his black boots.

Out of them all, Krawg's look was the most minimalist, clearly designed for function rather than appearance.

Designated as their bodyguard, the giant Ursite kept the plain black aesthetic of the original suit, only adding a few armored pieces here and there, like pauldrons, wrist and shin guards, and a narrow gorget that barely reined in the chaos of fur at his neck in order to affect a more military appearance. At his waist were a pair of blaster pistols, and a powerful bolt rifle was slung over his back.

Taj didn't expect their hosts to let him keep them, but they were largely for looks anyway. Thanks to Dent, the suits had been designed to absorb small weapons into their mass and make them part of the suit so the crew would always have a weapon handy should they need it. Taj grinned as she pictured the surprise when she and the others pulled weapons out of nowhere.

"Our escort is here," Dent announced. "The shuttle to the planet is docking now."

"Everyone know their role?" Taj asked.

"We're just ourselves," Torbon muttered. "Not like that's that hard to remember."

"You're supposed to be your *better* self," Taj corrected, wagging a finger his way. "Watch the cussing and speak properly so there's no confusion in translation."

"You sound like Mama Merr," Torbon complained, his shoulders slumped.

"Be grateful I'm not Mama or I'd bruise your knuckles for that lazy posture," she told him.

Lina chuckled. "I don't know how many times she popped his hands for slouching in his desk during lessons."

Torbon slipped his hands behind him, hiding them as he straightened. "More times than I want to remember," he admitted. "You better not start that gack."

"Language," Cabe warned, grinning the entire time.

Torbon sighed again. "This is gonna suck."

"Probably," Taj admitted with a laugh. "Now, let's go meet the shuttle and get on our way. Grom and the General are counting on us."

She started off toward the *Arrant*'s hangar bay, her heart pounding in her chest with excitement. This was what she'd always wanted, the opportunity to travel the universe and do more than chase down trrilacs and babysit wild balborans.

Taj had been given a chance to make a difference in the

universe, and she was gacking well gonna make the most of that opportunity.

The shuttle was an automated affair, barely doing more than acknowledging the crew's presence in a mechanized voice and ushering them into seats for the trip planet-side, for which Taj was grateful. She wanted a few more minutes to steel her nerves before the mission started in earnest, and she didn't need an audience for it.

The trip, fortunately, was short. On the ground, she sucked in a deep breath as the shuttle doors opened and the Zoranthian entourage appeared outside, all smiles and welcoming faces. She returned a smile of her own, letting her breath out easy.

She was ready.

Taj let Krawg and Dent lead the party out of the shuttle to cement the appearance that the two were servants of the royals inside. It felt weird doing so, she thought, but it was how things needed to be until they'd accomplished their mission and slipped away with Grom Hadar.

"Greetings," the lead representative of the Orgesse Clan called out as Dent and Krawg moved to stand in front of him. "I am Zel Ga'Vor, advisor to Queen Rilan Orgesse, matron saint of the Orgesse Clan. Welcome to Dulta, the capital city of Zoranthan."

Krawg stood his ground without so much as blinking, eyes scanning the tarmac, while Dent bowed and returned the greeting, giving Taj an opportunity to scope out the entourage without appearing overly anxious as she and the rest of the Furlorian crew filed out of the shuttle.

Zel was a wiry little man with graying hair, which was well on its way to balding. Strands fluttered across his pinkish scalp like flags waving in the wind. His eyes were narrow slits, all four of them, gleaming like yellow dots above his wide, grinning mouth. His nose was little more than a tiny bump squeezed between his mouth and double-eyes.

He wore long white robes with the Orgesse symbol embroidered over his heart, but that was the extent of his ornamentation. Simple sandals covered his feet and he had on no rings or jewelry of any kind, nothing to indicate rank or wealth. Taj wondered if that was normal here, and she was glad she'd chosen to minimize her accoutrements.

"Pleasure to meet you, Zel," Taj answered, turning up the wattage on her smile. While she and the others were meant to be royalty, their actual cover story was that they were the children of the true monarch of Krawlas, princes and princesses, and though they spoke for their people, General Reynolds had sold the Furlorians as a bit wayward, troubled.

He'd meant to give them a little wiggle room in the negotiations should they struggle to maintain appearances or screwed up in some other way.

Her thoughts fluttering, Taj examined the remainder of the entourage. All eight of them were far more militant than the austere representative who'd first greeted the crew. They wore form-fitting black body armor inter-woven with red highlights at the joints, but none of the soldiers—who were all female, Taj noted—wore helmets.

Their heads were shaved down to fuzz, and each had a downward-pointing triangle tattooed beneath their lower left eye.

Taj caught a glimpse of a shimmer in one of the soldier's upper eyes who glanced up at her, and she realized the soldiers wore an optical device similar to the one Dent had given the crew. She knew right away the soldier was scanning her just as Taj was examining the soldier, the optic taking in every detail and saving it for later use.

"The gathering of ladies behind me are Heltrol, the Orgesse Clan royal guard," Zel said, motioning to the array of soldiers. "They are here for your protection, so I'd advise doing what they ask."

The lead soldier stepped forward, the one Taj had noticed staring at her, and the woman offered a shallow nod.

"I am Commander Lei Rolkar, the queen's personal guard," she said, acknowledging each of the crew in turn, her gaze settling on Taj in the end. "If you will follow us to the vehicles, we will escort you to the palace." The woman gestured toward a row of three hovercraft idling a short distance away. "We must, however, insist upon claiming your weapons," she said, pausing before leading them off. "They will be returned to you upon your departure, of course."

"Of course," Taj mimicked, motioning for Krawg to hand over all of the weapons he'd openly carried out.

The giant Ursite grunted as if unhappy with the choice, but he did as he was compelled, passing the rifle to one of the soldiers first, followed by both pistols. A second soldier circled him, eyeing him up and down then glancing at the rest of the crew before finally offering a nod to her commander.

"Please, follow me," Rolkar told them, waving the crew on.

Zel smiled and matched their pace. "The queen will be thrilled to see you," he said as the crew climbed into the middle of the three vehicles.

To Taj's surprise, only Commander Rolkar and Zel climbed in with them, the representative closing the door behind them in the roomy vehicle and sitting across from them.

The rest of the soldiers climbed onto platforms Taj hadn't originally seen mounted along the outside of the vehicle. She heard the sullen thump of magnetic clamps taking hold and glanced out the forward window. Soldiers filed out of the other vehicle and did the same to the vehicle in front, and Taj caught a glimpse of more doing the same behind them.

Zel grinned. "It's a bit of a show of force and subterfuge at the same time," the rep explained, apparently seeing her confusion as the caravan started off. "While the journey to the palace is not overly long, it winds through a rather heavily-populated area of Dulta. Always best to be safe."

Krawg growled deep in his throat but said nothing, keeping up his role as the strong, silent guardian of the visiting royals.

Commander Rolkar grinned at him. "Worry not, we'll keep your charges safe, large one. We'd simply rather err on the side of caution than take a chance with your wellbeing."

"I presume the threat lies in the Orv and Talaz clans?" Dent asked, raising a manicured eyebrow.

"You've done your due diligence, I see," Rolkar replied, still grinning. "Them and others, yes."

Zel cleared his throat with a delicate cough and cut in. "The Orgesse Clan, the greatest of all the clans here on Zoranthan, has many enemies, in keeping with their status as world leaders," the rep explained, shrugging as if his revelation held as much weight as discussing the weather. "Orgesse has ruled Zoranthan for nearly a century, and the rival clans clamber and claw and strike out now and again to show their displeasure with their circumstances."

"They're hardly anything to worry about, truly," Rolkar stated. "It's been months since any of the other clans have lashed out in any way other than politically. They also have no idea you and your people have arrived on planet and have no reason to even look twice at a royal caravan," the commander went on. "As such, sit back and relax and enjoy the trip. We'll be at the palace shortly. Queen Rilan is looking forward to meeting with you."

"We're looking forward to meeting her, as well," Taj replied.

Torbon rolled his eyes when no one but Taj was looking, and she sneered at him.

Watch it, Torbon, she spoke in her head, letting the optic carry her message silently to him.

These things are so gacking cool, he fired back, not even bothering to acknowledge her warning.

Taj swallowed her frustration with Torbon and settled back into her seat, staring out the window as the city of Dulta crawled past. Zel rambled on, pointing out landmarks and various points of interest while the commander sat ramrod straight, the implant in her eye glinting, no doubt processing everything she saw.

"Over there is the Vitrol Arena, where special events occur and the lower classes fight nightly to entertain those more fortunate," Zel said, pointing out the window to the left of the crew.

Taj caught a glimpse of a huge, silver-domed building in the distance before the vehicle turned and a nearby shop blocked her view.

"And this is merchant's row," the representative continued as the caravan of vehicles weaved through the narrow streets surrounded on all sides by short, squat buildings. "Much of the—"

A massive explosion erupted ahead of the vehicle the crew rode in, the lead hovercraft going up in a ball of flame.

Zel gasped and covered his head, ducking low in his seat.

Torbon grunted, wide-eyed, and pointed at the flaming wreck burning ahead of them. "I'm thinking *that* might be a problem."

CHAPTER FOUR

"Bloody Rowl!" Lina shrieked as their vehicle slid in an attempt to brake, the front end colliding with the flaring wreckage of the lead vehicle with a jarring *thud*.

"Stay down!" Commander Rolkar shouted, grabbing Zel by his collar and pushing him to the floor. She muttered something under her breath that Taj didn't catch.

Krawg hovered over the crew, pinning them under him as another explosion erupted behind them, rattling the vehicle and sending spiderwebbed cracks all through the windows. The temperature rose in a flash, heat wafting over the crew.

Taj peeked past a furry armpit to see the Heltrol guards spilling off the platforms and fanning out, firing into the wafts of black smoke that clouded the streets and blocked Taj's view beyond a short distance.

Another explosion went off, closer this time, and shoved their vehicle further into the wreckage of the first. The last remaining hovercraft gyrated wildly, nearly tipping over. The crew were tossed like rocks shaken in a can. Grunts, yips, and groans sounded while Krawg did his best to protect them with his body.

"Stay here," Rolkar called out, kicking the side door open and leaping out, weapon in hand.

She fired off several blasts into the smoke and kicked the door shut behind her, taking up a defensive position outside alongside a handful of her people.

"Nothing to worry about, huh?" Cabe asked Zel, who cowered on the floor.

The representative shrugged, all four of his eyes looking wet as though he might burst into tears any moment. "They've been so quiet of late," he said, his voice cracking.

Blaster shots ricocheted off the vehicle, and Zel buried his face in the plush carpet, mumbling something in a language Taj's translator couldn't identify.

Glass shattered above them, raining down on their heads.

Gack, Taj shouted across their mental comm link, furious that they'd surrendered their obvious weapons to the Heltrol soldiers.

She hadn't expected them to be attacked en route to the palace, and she didn't want anyone knowing that she and her people were armed and armored. She wanted that to be a surprise in case they needed an unexpected advantage.

Taj caught a flicker of motion outside and spied a force of ragtag soldiers closing on the vehicle. The men were dressed in robes and fought with aggressive zeal. The Heltrol engaged them, but it was clear the royal guard was outnumbered. Blaster fire sounded all around as more attackers joined the first.

We can't just sit here, Taj told the others. *We're an easy target cooped up in this vehicle.*

Not to mention those flames are getting a little too close for comfort, Cabe said, gesturing toward the front of the vehicle where telltale flickers of orangish-red spit sparks through the cracks in the window. The armored glass began to melt under the pressure.

One of the Heltrol soldiers was struck by a barrage of blaster fire and slammed into the side of the vehicle. She slumped out of sight, and Taj saw a second soldier drop a moment after, spatters of blood dotting the vehicle. Commander Rolkar screamed something incomprehensible and she and her soldiers pushed forward, disappearing into the swirling black smoke, firing their weapons as they went.

Gack it, Taj muttered across the link. *I don't know about you guys, but this doesn't feel right to me. We need to get out of here and defend ourselves without anyone seeing what we're capable of.*

She nudged Krawg aside, using the suit's system to increase her strength, grateful that the armor didn't need to look like armor to maintain its normal functions.

The Ursite flopped over onto Zel, dramatically driving an elbow into the base of the man's skull and knocking the representative unconscious where he sat hunched on the floor.

"Oops," Krawg mumbled, and Taj hoped the monarchy hadn't installed cameras in the vehicle because there was no way Krawg's maneuver looked anything remotely like an accident. At least the rep was no longer a witness to what they were doing, though.

Don't alter your uniforms or draw weapons unless you absolutely have to, Taj told the crew as Dent went to the door and eased it open. *Stay in character.*

That's the kind of thing that's gonna get us shot, Torbon complained.

Maybe, Taj replied, *but do it anyway. And drag Zel out so the fire doesn't get him. Wouldn't be a good start to the trip if we let him burn up.*

Yeah, because the rest of this is wonderful, Cabe complained.

Between the swirl of smoke, Taj caught a glimpse of movement outside, a wave of dark shadows moving through an alley toward them, but she couldn't make out the red and black of the Heltrol.

Trouble's coming, she told the crew.

Taj leapt out of the vehicle, past Dent, and rolled across the ground, snatching up one of the pistols the fallen Heltrol had dropped. She familiarized herself with the gun as quickly as she could, her optic display simplifying the process by feeding her the schematics, and she loosed a barrage of fire in the direction of the approaching enemy she couldn't see very clearly.

And then she suddenly could, the world clearing before her eyes.

She regretted the clarity immediately.

I've remotely activated your advanced vision optics, Dent said over the link, explaining the sudden, unexpected shift.

"I see," she muttered. Literally.

Gack!

Something in the neighborhood of twenty robed soldiers stormed toward the stalled vehicle and Taj and her crew. They were clearly locals, wearing hooded masks that covered their faces but left their four eyes visible. Their outfits were plain, black, and unidentifiable without any markings, and all of them carried rifles of some sort.

Now that she could target them effectively, Taj's next burst of fire dropped one and staggered another, but the attackers were too spread out to hit easily.

Fortunately, the rest of the crew joined her a moment later and collected more fallen weapons, plenty of them lying about. Bursts of energy ripped past her and tore into the charging enemy, slowing their advance as the attackers reacted, but not stopping them completely.

They came forward with a purpose.

Taj could hear the battle echoing all around her. Rolkar's voice cut through the din of war as though she were off in the distance, making Taj wonder how the woman intended to protect them if she was nowhere near to do so.

Guess we need to do it ourselves, she thought, not sending that comment to her companions.

"Move there," she called out, pushing back against the crew and maneuvering them around the corner, putting a wall in between them and the attackers, if only for a few seconds. Lina dragged the unconscious Zel behind her, setting him against the wall to their backs.

Taj glanced toward the last vehicle in the caravan to see that it, too, had been engulfed in flames, black smoke billowing through its shattered windows. A small number of Heltrol bodies littered the street around the vehicle, but Taj didn't count more than four or five.

Where are the rest of them? she asked herself.

There wasn't time to ponder the answer as the squad of attackers rounded the corner, taking aim at the vehicle as they ran toward it. They were clearly unable to see past the smoke, Taj held up her fist to stop her crew from firing right away and drawing their attention. She crouched, motioning for the others to follow her movements.

Wait a second, she warned, trailing the attackers with her gun as they crept to encircle the vehicle. *Let them all get into the open.*

Seconds passed slowly as Taj waited. She wanted nothing more than to blast these guys in the back and mow them down, but she knew there was something wrong and she wasn't going to take any chances. There were simply too many enemies, all too well-prepared, to have made the attack one of opportunity. Someone had to have known the vehicles would be coming this way, and it didn't bode well for the Furlorians that an enemy would have such advanced knowledge of their arrival.

She looked into the distance again, still unable to see Commander Rolkar and her soldiers despite the continued sounds of fighting going on around them.

A niggling boulder of doubt sat hard in her stomach. Rolkar hadn't just left *them* to their fate, she'd abandoned Zel, too. That didn't sit right with Taj.

"Now!" she called, reverting to speech out of habit once the group of assailants cleared the corner.

She tapped the trigger of her borrowed weapon over and over as the attackers spread out before them, backs turned. They were caught off guard, clearly having believed their target—be it the Furlorians or Zel, Taj hadn't yet determined—were still in the vehicle and the way had been cleared.

Unfortunately for them, that wasn't the case at all.

Bolts ripped into the unarmored backs of the assailants, ripping them apart without a hint of mercy. The attackers grunted and screamed and fell beneath the barrage, the crew taking them out before any of them could process what was happening and dive for cover.

A few moments later, the assailants were on the ground, dead or dying.

The sound of fighting grew weaker in the distance soon after, and Taj spied one of the masked men roll to his side and start to crawl beneath the vehicle as she surveyed the scene. His tattered robes dragged behind him.

"Watch the rest of them," she told her crew, gesturing to the last of the dying enemies.

She hissed low in her throat and ran over to the fleeing man, grabbing him by his leg and yanking him out before he managed to get more than half his body under cover. He cursed and shouted, but he couldn't break free of her grip.

"Where do you think you're going?" she snarled, baring her teeth in his face as she pressed the barrel of her gun to his temple. He froze then, and Taj whipped the mask off his head so she could look him in the eyes.

Well, in a couple of them, at least.

"Who sent you?" she shouted, bombarding the survivor with questions. "Who are you after? Why are you here? What's all this about?"

The Zoranthian snarled, shaking his head in defiance

and saying nothing. A trickle of blood ran from his mouth, down his chin, and pattered to his chest. One of his four eyes was bloodshot and looked in a different direction than the rest, swimming about in its socket.

Taj glared at the man, taking in the thick scar that ran from his scalp, across his wayward eye, and all the way to his cheekbone. It looked like a crescent moon, the puckered skin silvery with sweat.

The rest of the crew circled Taj, keeping watch on the remainder of the assailants, most of whom had surrendered to their wounds and had stopped moving. Only a few still twitched, but that was short-lived. Silence settled over the group as Taj willed the survivor to talk, her eyes boring into him.

"Tell me why you're here," she pressed, though it was clear the man had no intention of giving up any information.

Right then, Commander Rolkar reappeared, a dozen of her Heltrol soldiers at her back. They burst through the smoke, weapons bared, racing toward the crew screaming.

"Everyone freeze!" Rolkar shouted, her gun sweeping the area. The Heltrol formed a half-circle around the Furlorians, weapons pointed at them.

Taj growled at the woman. "Seriously?" she snapped, stepping away from her captive for just a second to complain to the commander.

That distraction was all it took.

There was a shuffle and a *clank*, and a small, round device clattered across the road, bouncing into the pile of bodies littering the street.

"Grenade!" a soldier screamed, and everyone scattered. Rolkar dove behind the abandoned vehicle.

Taj cursed under her breath and leapt, hitting the ground and rolling away from the weapon her captive had unleashed. The rest of the crew scrambled right along with her, piling up over Zel. Krawg triggered his armor's external defenses, a force field shimmering around him as he threw his arms around the crew and pulled them in tight, his back to the grenade.

The device exploded a moment later.

Taj felt a wallop of energy wash over them, Krawg holding his ground mightily as shrapnel pattered across the energy shield he'd thrown up. The Ursite groaned under the pressure, and then his weight slumped down over them as the shockwave passed. He let out a loud sigh, and Taj felt his weight ease up a little. His shield wavered and fell away.

"That was rather climactic," he muttered, clambering to his feet a moment later and letting the rest of the crew get up.

"How did you know there was a force field on the armor?" Lina asked Krawg, her ears pinned to the side of her head.

He shrugged his furry shoulders. "I didn't."

Taj's eyes went wide as she stared at him. "Wait. What do you mean you didn't know?"

I activated it, Dent said across the mental link. *Krawg was quite the hero, but I figured he might need some assistance since his fur, however matted and water resistant it might be, likely wouldn't be much protection from shrapnel. The armor would have certainly helped in his heroic quest, but I figured it best to be certain.*

"Never know until you try, right, Krawg?" Torbon asked, chuckling.

The hulking Ursite grunted. Taj didn't know if that was him agreeing with Torbon or not. Either way, she was glad Dent had equipped them for their mission and had the presence of mind to involve himself even if he hadn't actually informed them of all the things the suits could do.

She would need to correct that oversight soon.

"Are you all right?" Commander Rolkar asked the crew, rounding the vehicle. Her soldiers joined her. She walked over, subconsciously dusting layers of grit off her armor as if it was the biggest issue she faced.

"No thanks to—" Cabe started, baring his teeth, but Taj elbowed him in the side, shutting him up before he could finish.

"We're fine, thank you," Taj answered, handing her borrowed weapon to the commander as if it disgusted her. "We're just lucky to have found a few of these *things* lying about that we could use to defend ourselves." While Taj hadn't meant to be snippy, she couldn't help but let a tiny bit of fire leak into her tone. She caught herself, though, and stepped back into the role of princess before she let the commander have it and she ruined everything. "Our security man here did most of the work, fortunately," she said, motioning toward Krawg. "We're not much for gunfights, to be fair."

Commander Rolkar's eyes narrowed, and Taj wasn't sure if the woman believed the act or not. "Yes, it is fortunate your security detail was with you. Things got a bit chaotic out here."

She glanced around at the smoldering bodies of the assailants the Furlorians had taken down, parts scattered all over thanks to the grenade's explosion. The woman sighed unexpectedly, the hardness of her features giving way to frustration.

"The zealots lured us away," she explained, gesturing toward the other side of the wrecked vehicle where she'd been, her voice actually wavering as she spoke. "They've never come at us with so many, nor have they used these types of tactics before, splitting their forces and coordinating their efforts. They normally come at us in a horde, all at once, straight on like maniacs. This, however, was... quite different."

Taj narrowed her eyes, staring at the commander as if she could suss out whether the woman was being honest or not. She was disappointed, though, unable to determine anything for certain, but now wasn't the time to question the commander, she realized.

Taj and her people had a mission to accomplish, and they needed to get on with it. "Is there another vehicle we can—"

"Wait!" Rolkar called out, clearly realizing something was amiss and cutting Taj off. She glanced around, head on a swivel. "Where is Zel?"

"Over there," Cabe told her, pointing to where the representative had been set over by the wall.

"He was...uh, stunned during the fight," Krawg clarified, though he looked away like a child caught stuffing a furry hand in a cookie jar. "He's okay, though. Promise."

Smooth, Lina said across the mental link, laughing at the Ursite.

"Our servant, Dent, pulled him out of the vehicle to keep him safe," Taj said, still trying to sell their role as royalty.

The commander didn't seem to care either way.

She went over to Zel and checked him, nodding as she assured herself the rep was not seriously wounded. Taj watched Rolkar, distrusting of the woman given how she'd run off in the middle of the fight, but Taj couldn't determine if the move had been on purpose or simply an error in the fog of war. Either was possible, and Taj didn't like not knowing.

She seemed to genuinely care about the rep's wellbeing.

A quiet hum drew Taj from her questions, though, and she glanced up to see a tiny drone hovering a short distance away. A second one joined it a moment later. Red dots gleamed on the faces of the drones, and they kept their distance.

"Ma'am," one of the soldiers called out, getting the commander's attention.

Rolkar glanced over her shoulder and growled. "Damn it!" She tapped her comm and muttered something about a pickup.

The crew stared at the drones.

"What are those?" Taj asked.

"Automated news drones," Rolkar answered with a snarl. She motioned to the wreckage of the caravan. "Those things are the bane of my existence. They show up everywhere you don't want them to," the commander grunted. "Our little adventure here is going to be on every channel within minutes, and Queen Rilan will know what happened even sooner."

Taj growled under her breath and spun around, facing away from the camera, though she realized it was too late. Each and every one of the crew had stood still and looked directly at the drones, meaning all their faces would be broadcast across the planet for everyone to see in short order.

There would be no sneaking around town looking for answers now.

So much for stealth, Dent said, mirroring her thoughts.

The realization sinking in with the rest of the crew as the AI spoke, they all turned their backs to the cameras as inconspicuously as they could, not that it mattered at that point.

That's it, Torbon muttered over the link. *We're gacked.*

Taj bit back a sigh. She hated when Torbon was right.

That was when another caravan of vehicles arrived, zooming to a halt before them, dozens of Heltrol soldiers arrayed on the outsides of the hovercraft. Taj noticed a crowd of people gathering at the periphery, watching what was going on as intently as the news drones.

It looked like the whole town had come out to see what had happened now that the gunfire was over.

The commander ushered them into one of the newly-arrived vehicles. Her soldiers carried Zel and stuffed him into the hovercraft after them. The representative's eyes fluttered and finally opened as the new caravan shot off. He looked around the cabin, taking in his surroundings with a glassy stare.

"I must have fallen asleep," he said while rubbing the

back of his head and trying to sit upright, not doing a good job of it. It was clear he wasn't entirely sure where he was still. "My sincerest apologies. I don't know what came over me. I must be getting old." He moaned as he touched a tender spot on his scalp right where Krawg had clobbered him. "Looks like I hit my head somewhere along the way, too. Oh dear."

The crew stifled a chuckle at the man's confusion, but Taj was grateful he hadn't realized Krawg had knocked him out and that the Ursite hadn't done any permanent damage.

That was the only good thing to happen so far, she thought as she replayed the encounter in her head. Once more, she stared out the window and watched the city fly by as she contemplated the crew's mission and how she could fix things before the mission was blown.

Sadly, she was still in the dark as to what was going on and whether the attack on the caravan had been an attempt on their lives or something else entirely. There were simply far too many questions she didn't have answers to, and she hated it.

Her gaze rested on Commander Rolkar, watching as the woman tended to Zel, who kept his head down and remained quiet. Taj's earlier suspicion reared up again, only adding to her confusion.

Something was going on, but Taj had no clue as to what it was.

She hated the feeling.

Hey! Rowl knows, it can only get better from here, Torbon said with a smile, clearly seeing her pondering the situation and trying to reassure her.

Taj sighed.

Way to jinx us, gackboy, she replied over the link and slumped into her seat.

Now that Torbon had invoked the catty god and drawn her attention, Taj was sure things were going to get worse.

CHAPTER FIVE

Taj hated when she was right even more than she
hated when Torbon was.

Things *had* gotten worse.

As soon as the crew arrived at the Orgesse Palace,
Rolkar ordered the Heltrol to collect the remaining
weapons the crew had held onto, and they were marched
through the palace with only the barest of cordiality.

Commander Rolkar waved a hand at various sights
along their route—from family portraits where a young
queen sat stoically alongside her two sisters and her
brother while her parents hovered above, to an extensive
art gallery they passed in a blur without any real chance to
gawk—as she raced them to a suite of guest chambers on
the far side of the palace.

As soon as they arrived, the crew were hurried inside,
not allowed to ask any questions until the doors were shut
and locked behind them, leaving them alone with the

commander. Her entourage of Heltrol guards remained outside the door, and Taj could hear them pacing.

"I thought we were going to see Queen Rilan," Taj complained, turning to face the commander with her hands on her hips. She was starting to enjoy the impudent aspect of her role.

"You will," Rolkar answered, but the look on her face spoke of tempered expectations. "I need to speak with the queen and make arrangements for the meeting first. Until then, you will be confined to your chambers as a safety precaution."

"Like with the caravan?" Cabe asked, sneering.

Taj thought to rein him in for a second, not wanting to offend the commander more than she might have already, but as she thought about it, she realized that pampered royalty angle was perfect. Them being placed on what amounted to house arrest would most assuredly piss off a group of spoiled royal children.

"I apologize—" Rolkar began, but Taj cut her off with a sniping tone.

"You intend to lock us in our rooms like recalcitrant children then?" Taj asked, letting the words come out in a snotty growl.

Then she caught herself wondering if she'd used the word *recalcitrant* correctly and realized she should probably stop with the big words before she made herself look foolish.

"Only for a short time while, I assure—"

"So, the answer is yes?" Taj countered, not letting the commander explain. "This is unacceptable, Commander Rolkar," she argued, stomping her foot for emphasis.

"We are guests of the Orgesse Clan, not prisoners," Lina added, catching on to what Taj was going for and piling on.

"Does this mean we were the target of your opponents?" Dent asked, joining in, subtly prodding for information. "It would appear so by the way my lords are being treated. Why else would you lock them away so quickly and absolutely?"

Commander Rolkar sighed, her shoulders slumping. Whatever her training might have been, Taj was pretty certain it wasn't in public relations. She felt sorry for the woman for a moment, but then remembered she'd left them to be attacked out in the streets, and Taj was annoyed all over again, for real this time.

"Unacceptable!" Taj growled.

"I-I don't know," Rolkar answered Dent after a moment's pause where she clearly struggled to keep her composure. "That is part of what I must determine before I can say anymore. Until then—"

"Surely you know whether or not we were the target of these base ruffians," Taj shouted.

Cabe glanced at her, eyebrow raised. *Base ruffians?*

It's called acting, she answered, lifting her nose into the air and giving a sullen sniff as if she'd been attacked by a holo-critic.

It's called overacting, Torbon countered, and Dent nodded his agreement.

Taj sniffed imperiously, glaring their direction before turning it back on the commander.

"These terrorists," Taj corrected, jabbing a finger in Rolkar's direction, "clearly had an agenda, Commander. I want to know how they knew we were coming, why we were targeted, and I want to know now!" she huffed. "This is going to affect our negotiations, I assure you."

Rolkar stiffened at the obvious threat. "Please, allow me to speak with the queen and our intelligence officers before you make any decisions." She backed toward the door as if worried about turning her back on the Furlorians. "I will have the servants bring you food and refreshments. Please, rest and relax for now," she told them, raising her hands in clear hopes of pacifying them. "I will appraise you once I've spoken with the queen, and we know more of what happened."

The commander didn't give the crew time to argue as she whipped the door to their chambers open and stepped outside in a rush. But before she managed to close the door, Taj spied a handful of the Heltrol soldiers outside, the women clearly having been stationed there.

Whether they were there to protect the crew or guard them was up in the air.

Rolkar closed the door behind her, and Taj heard a heavy bolt slide shut outside, pretty much answering her question.

"Did she just lock us in?" Cabe asked.

Taj nodded and went to say something, but Lina held up a finger, motioning for silence.

"I'm pretty sure she did," Torbon answered, not paying any attention to Lina's gestures.

Lina sighed and smacked him upside the back of his head, hissing in his face. Torbon winced and glared at the engineer as she went over to the door.

"What'd I do?" Torbon asked.

Shut up, the crew bombarded him over the mental link.

I'm looking for bugs, Lina clarified as she strolled the perimeter of the room, slipping into the bedrooms and scanning each with a device built into the armor.

I doubt a place this fancy has bugs, Torbon thought with indignance. *I don't even see a hint of dust. They keep this place clean. I need to hire their maid service.*

At least he's pretty? Taj said.

Sadly, he's not even that, Lina said, grinning at Torbon's denseness.

Torbon's eyes narrowed, apparently finally cluing in that they were making fun of him. He snorted and crossed his arms over his chest.

The rest of the crew waited quietly until Lina finished scanning the chambers for listening devices, and then they gathered in the next room over, away from the door so they couldn't be overheard by the guards outside. Lina and Taj flopped down on the bed, Cabe and Torbon grabbed chairs, and Dent remained standing.

Krawg loudly announced he was going to find food.

"She said she'd send some soon," Cabe told the Ursite.

Krawg shrugged. "That doesn't mean there isn't already some here," he argued as he left the room. "Besides, someone needs to watch the door in case someone comes sneaking in."

Cabe didn't bother to argue.

"Never mind him," Taj said, drawing their attention to her. "We've got bigger things to worry about than Krawg's appetite."

"I'm pretty hungry, too," Torbon said, raising his hand.

"Let me clarify." Taj sighed. "We have bigger things to worry about than Krawg's *or* your appetite."

"I beg to differ," Torbon argued, shaking his head.

"Anyway," Taj went on, ignoring Torbon's exaggerated rubbing of his stomach, "the mission has clearly gone south in a big way already."

"That's an understatement," Cabe replied, slumping into his seat.

"No, I believe it's a fairly adequate assessment of the current circumstances," Dent said. "An understatement would be if Taj said things didn't look good."

"Your sarcasm detector is clearly out of alignment," Cabe muttered.

"I don't have a sarcasm detect— Oh! I get it," the AI answered, grinning.

Cabe chuckled. "I think I liked you better when your brain was broken. At least you had a sense of humor then."

Taj waved the pair to silence. They didn't have time for banter.

"Stow it, guys," she told them. "We need to focus."

A knock on the front door interrupted them, and Krawg called out a second later. "Food's here!"

The Ursite let the servants in, who filed into the room with several large serving carts covered in a variety of food and drink. A mélange of delicious smells wafted into the room, and Torbon leapt from his chair and followed his nose, whiskers twitching in anticipation.

Taj sighed and waved for Lina to follow him. *Make sure they didn't bug the carts, please.*

Lina nodded and chased after Torbon. The servants vacated the room quickly after their delivery, and once more Taj heard the bolt being drawn outside, locking the crew in their quarters, which sent a chill down Taj's spine.

She didn't like the idea of being a prisoner, even if they were capable of breaking out any time they wanted. It didn't sit well with her.

Lina returned a moment later, giving Taj a thumbs up.

"We're good," she said, dropping back down on the bed beside Taj. "No bugs on the carts."

Taj gritted her teeth at the news, realizing the lack of listening devices only added more confusion to the mix. "I wonder if this means we can trust Commander Rolkar," she wondered aloud.

"Her disappearance after making a point about our safety did seem a bit suspicious," Dent answered. "Contrary, at the very least."

"But the lack of bugs in the room, a room they had plenty of time to prepare ahead of time, kinda throws any suspicion of her into question," Lina countered. "Who doesn't at least make a show of bugging a political visitor's room? That's Royal Subterfuge 101, right?"

"Maybe they didn't expect us to survive long enough to make it here," Cabe said, shrugging.

"That's a sobering thought," Taj replied, "but it doesn't make any sense. Why let us come at all if they're just gonna kill us as soon as we land? And what does killing us gain them?"

"I don't know, but I'm thinking you don't bring that many people unless you plan to kill someone," Cabe argued. "Maybe the Orgesse wanted to make a show of it, something they could use against their rivals. This was a damn big public spectacle, which is gonna end up all over the news. That has to have some value to them in the political arena."

"If that was the case, they could have just as easily let word of our arrival slip and allow the other clans to take us out in space before we even landed," Taj shot back. "No doubt that would have given the Orgesse Clan plenty of political options and would have saved them the effort of losing vehicles and soldiers."

"The assailants were probably after Zel," Lina said. "That would make more sense given everything we know about the politics here. We were probably seen as collateral damage by the Orgesse enemies, whichever group it was, nothing more than an excuse to get at the queen's representative."

Taj exhaled hard and flopped onto her back on the bed, rubbing her eyes. "None of this is helping us any," she mumbled. "There are too many damn questions without any answers."

"I think maybe we're letting paranoia and ego get in the way of rational thought," Dent said, derailing all the speculation. "All of this could be a coincidence, nothing more. Rival factions seeing an opportunity to go after the queen's caravan to make a point regardless of who might be in it, much like what Lina said but without a bigger incentive. In the end, the attack might have had nothing to do with us."

"But that's less dramatic than there being a plot to murder us all," Torbon mumbled as he returned to the room, munching on the cooked wing of some kind of exotic avian. A sheen of grease coated his whiskers, and he licked his lips. "Taj can't overact if everything's just a coincidence and no one cares about us."

"I can still shoot you, though," Taj pointed out.

Torbon reclaimed his seat and shrugged at her threat, too busy gnawing on the bone to muster a reply.

"Where does that leave us if that's the case?" Lina asked.

"Right where we were to begin with," Taj replied, letting a sigh slip out. "Confused as gack-all, our faces plastered all over the planet, and no idea where Grom Hadar is."

Taj's lack of experience in matters of subterfuge frustrated her, though she didn't want to admit it. She'd spent her whole life dealing with the simplest of politics possible, Mama Merr and Beaux setting the law and shutting down their opposition without much more than a few verbal jabs. They hadn't had any true rivals to their rule.

As such, Taj hadn't experienced political backstabbing, for which she was grateful, but she wished she'd had more time to study the interplay between the Orgesse Clan and their rivals before they'd come. However, there was no point in worrying about it now, seeing how little she understood.

She felt it best to move on with the mission and hope she was just being paranoid like Dent had said.

"We need to focus on the task at hand and track down Grom Hadar before anything happens to him," she told the crew. "But now we need a new plan seeing how we're stuck here and our hosts have planted guards at the front door."

While the original plan had been fairly simple—use the cover of their visit with the Orgesse as a way to go into town and seek out Grom's last known location and see what could be found there—the circumstances had changed.

Between being locked in the palace and the whole city, possibly the whole planet, having seen their faces, which inexorably linked them to the Orgesse Clan, putting a target on their heads with regards to the other clans, their plan was shot all to gack.

"I'm thinking we wait it out and see what happens once we get an audience with the queen," Torbon said, pausing for only a moment before returning to his meal. "Maybe things aren't as bad as we're making them out to be."

"You just want to stay close to the food," Lina told him, rolling her eyes.

"No sense letting it all go to waste," he argued.

"We can't wait that long," Taj said with a growl.

She could picture Grom Hadar out there, hiding and hoping the Federation found him before something bad happened. She could picture being him, could feel his fear and uncertainty, and she hated it. There was no way she would let him down. She had to believe he was alive and in hiding. Otherwise, everything they were going through had no purpose. Unless it was a live training mission and there was no Grom Hadar. She wondered if the Federation was playing them, seeing what the Furlorians were made of.

"I have an idea," she said.

"Is it a good one?" Torbon asked.

Taj shrugged. "I guess we'll find out soon enough."

CHAPTER SIX

S kol Arduin watched the newscast as it played across the pair of view screens set in the wall across from his seat. He clenched his fists and did his best to swallow his frustration at what he saw.

He failed miserably.

His men moved quietly around the room behind him, doing their best to stay out of sight where they wouldn't inadvertently become the target of his wrath. They knew exactly what would happen to them if they didn't.

He admired their wisdom, even if it meant he would have to wait a little longer in order to vent the fury that churned in his belly. Skol could wait, he told himself.

He *would* wait.

So, rather than take his anger out on those doing their best to avoid antagonizing him, he gnawed at his lower lip and mustered all the patience he could manage, his foot tapping the floor in a rhythmic *thump*.

And just when he'd decided he really couldn't wait any

longer, Vetrus, his right-hand man, came over and stood alongside his chair.

"Blas has returned," Vetrus said, the man's voice making each word sound like he was spitting out glass.

"About damn time," Skol barked, fighting the urge to jump up and storm off after the fool. Vetrus's presence helped rein him in, but it did nothing to temper his rage.

A few moments later, there was a shuffle at the front of the room and a handful of his men escorted Blas into the room, making sure he had no choice but to march directly up to where Skol sat.

Skol met the man's three good eyes, a grin peeling Skol's lips back as he spied the trickle of sweat that ran in the groove of the man's scar.

"You've made the news, Blas," Skol told him, gesturing toward the view screens that replayed the aftermath of the battle in an endless loop. "You know what I always say about that, don't you?"

Blas swallowed hard, offering up a plaintive nod. "Never let anyone film our failure," he said barely above a whisper.

Skol wagged a finger at him. "No, that's not exactly what I say, is it?"

Blas trembled but said nothing.

Skol drew in a deep breath and let it out slow, climbing to his feet. He drew forward slowly, coming to stand eye-to-eye with Blas.

"Never let anyone film *your* failure, is what I always say, Blas," Skol corrected. "You remember now?"

Blas offered up a pathetic nod.

"I say that, of course, because *your* failure doesn't define *me,*" Skol went on. "Except when it does, of course." Skol grinned and reached out, clasping Blas's shoulder with one of his hands, giving it a hard squeeze. "And this—" His eyes motioned to the screens. "—this is damn definitive, Blas."

Skol released him and returned to his chair, dropping down with a grunt.

"Imagine my absolute joy when I turned on the news to see all my men dead and scattered in pieces all over the street while those I sent you to collect stare at the camera as if they're mocking me for trusting such an incompetent shit such as yourself," he said. "How do you think that makes me feel, Blas?"

"Not good," Blas answered, squeezing the words out.

"Damn right," Skol agreed, thumping a fist against the arm of his chair. "Not good, Blas. Not good at all."

"They...they put up a fight," Blas managed. "I-it wasn't as easy as he said it would be. They—"

"It-it-it was too hard," Skol mocked, mimicking Blas's stutter. "H-he s-said it would be easy."

Blas withered under Skol's glare.

Skol growled at his subordinate's cowardice and jumped back to his feet.

"That's why I sent a damn army with you, Blas," Skol shouted, stomping over to loom in front of Blas once more, his heavy-booted steps echoing through the room. "An army that is now dead and blown into gory little pieces that the news is showing over and over." He jabbed a finger into Blas's chest. "Now tell me, Blas, did the rich little royal kids blow my army up? Did the Heltrol bitches?"

Blas shook his head, tremors rattling through him as he did.

"No, I didn't think so. It's not like people run around carrying grenades with them all the time. Except you, of course," Skol told him, letting out a weary sigh. "You blew them up trying to get away, didn't you?"

"T-they were already dead before I threw the grenade, I swear," Blas answered, choking out the words. "T-those cats killed them. Shot them down from behind, butchered them without mercy."

"Did they now?" Skol asked, inching even closer. He could smell the fear wafting off Blas as he did. "Those waify-looking balls of fur killed my army?"

Blas nodded so hard he nearly stumbled, throwing himself off balance.

Skol straightened and shoved the man out of his face. He twisted his head sideways, popping the bones in his neck. Vibrations rattled down his spine. He wanted so badly to strangle someone right then.

"The cats killed my men?" he asked again, Blas falling over himself to assure Skol that they had.

Skol turned away and returned to his chair, pacing in front of it, rubbing at his stubbled chin.

"I should kill you right now, Blas," Skol told him, turning back around and walking to stand in front of the wreck of a man that was Blas. "I *should*...but I won't."

Blas dropped to his knees and blubbered his thanks, tears and spit spattering the floor before him.

"I actually believe you," Skol said, resting a hand on Blas's head. "I'd been led to think the latest Orgesse visitors were nothing more than royal brats, a means to a quick ransom like all the others before them, but maybe I was wrong."

Skol motioned for his men to lift Blas to his feet. They complied, and Blas did his best to stay there on his own, swaying side to side as though he might collapse again despite his reprieve.

"I need you to deliver a message for me, Blas. Can you do that?" Skol asked.

"Y-yes!" Blas replied, his face a river of snot and tears.

Skol sighed. "Here's what I need you to do," he said, filling in Blas on the details of his message. Then, before he let the man go, he took a good look at the ruin standing before him. "Clean yourself up first," he told him, motioning to his men. "Get him out of here."

Once Blas was escorted out, Skol turned back to Vetrus, who had stood his ground alongside Skol's chair with a statue's stoicism.

"I want to see him," Skol said.

Vetrus nodded and spun on a heel, marching off. Skol followed, his right-hand man leading him to an unassuming set of doors hidden in the shadows at the back of the room. The doors hissed open as the pair arrived, and they stepped inside. The doors closed, and the elevator sank into the floor.

A few moments later they had arrived, and the doors eased open. Skol followed Vetrus out of the elevator and down a long, dimly-lit corridor that reeked of copper and wet stone. The air grew colder as they walked, and Skol could see the barest hint of his breath billowing with every step.

They passed rows of thick, steel doors as they made their way to the end of the hall, where another heavy door loomed. Vetrus halted in front of it and set a hand upon an access plate on the wall beside it. A green light flickered, scanning the man's palm, and then there was a loud thump as a series of bolts came undone.

Vetrus pulled the door open with a grunt, and a wave of fetid air escaped the room and washed over Skol. He grunted and turned his face from the cloying scent, making sure to breathe through his mouth to avoid the worst of it.

"He smells quite ripe," Skol muttered, shaking his head. "Perhaps it's time to pluck him, Vetrus. What do you say?"

Vetrus chuckled, the sound like shards of glass grinding together, and slipped into the room. Skol went in after him and spied the wretched heap that he'd caught a whiff of before he'd even entered the room.

Curled up in the far corner of the small, sparse cell, which contained nothing but its prisoner, an emaciated man hunkered down and stared out at Skol, all four of his eyes narrow, yellow slits gleaming in the darkness.

"You're looking good, Grom," Skol told the prisoner, moving over to stand in the middle of the cell. "Prison suits you."

Grom spit at Skol, but the wet missile barely escaped his lips.

Skol shrugged. "Maybe he's not ready quite yet."

Vetrus stepped forward in a blur of motion and back-handed Grom, slamming his head into the wall and causing the prisoner to cry out and topple over onto his hands and knees.

"Show some respect, Hadar, or I'll carve your eyes out of your skull," Vetrus threatened.

Blood dripped from Grom's mouth and dotted the floor

beneath him. He sat back on his haunches, one hand clutching the back of his skull.

Skol raised his arm and tapped on a device, a small screen brightening and illuminating the gloomy cell. An image of the Furlorians appeared on the screen, taken directly from the news. They stared directly at the camera, and Skol clasped Grom by the back of his scraggly hair and shoved the screen in his face.

"Who are these people?"

Grom shook his head, barely glancing at the screen.

"Are these your Federation contacts?" Skol pressed, tightening his grip and forcing Grom to look more closely at the image before him. "Are they here for you?"

Grom Hadar snarled and bared his teeth, stained red from Vetrus's blow. "No one's coming for me," he spat. "No one cares."

"Oh, I don't believe that, Grom," Skol told him. "We found evidence of your discussions with the Etheric Federation and its people, all behind the backs of your supposed Orgesse allies."

Skol released him, and Grom slumped to the floor, still glaring.

"If we hadn't, we'd have turned you over to the Heltrol for a tidy sum of credits, and you'd already be free of us," Skol said. "Now look at you, trapped in a dirty cell and slowly starving. Is this how you want to go out, Grom? A skeletal wretch dying in anonymity in an underground prison?"

Grom straightened as best he could, biting back a grunt. "It's better than giving in to you," he mustered, blood-flecked spittle flying with every word.

Skol shook his head. "I don't think even *you* believe that," he replied. "We will break you eventually, and you will tell us everything you intended to tell the Federation about the Orgesse Clan soon enough."

Skol took a step back, grinning like a feral hound.

"And if you won't, your feline friends most certainly will."

Grom snarled and leapt at Skol, fists raised, but Vetrus intercepted him.

A brutal punch to the prisoner's jaw sent him sprawling. Grom crashed into the wall and groaned as he fell to the cold, stone floor. A small pool of crimson blood formed beneath his drooling mouth. He raised a trembling hand toward Skol, muttering a curse that could be determined only by the curl of his upper lip and its tone.

"You betray yourself with your actions, Grom," Skol announced. "That you would risk injury to defend these off-worlders tells me that they might well be important to you after all. That's good enough for me at this point to insist they be brought before me."

He motioned with a thumb over his shoulder.

"You'll likely have neighbors soon, so think well on what you plan to tell them as we will most assuredly let them know they are here because of you."

Skol spun on his heel and started for the door, pausing when he reached it. He looked to Grom once more, then turned his attention on Vetrus.

"Patch him up so we don't lose him before we acquire his accomplices," he told his second, offering a toothy grin. "Then break him a little."

Skol chuckled and left the room, leaving his captive in

the cruel hands of Vetrus, knowing full well the joy his man felt at doing harm.

"Just a little, Vetrus," Skol called out as he left the hall and returned to the elevator.

He drew in a deep breath of moist air, glad to be free of the stink of the cell and its hostage. Skol rode the elevator, reveling in the silence as his thoughts whirled, and he plotted how to get his hands on the Federation operatives that had come to rescue Grom Hadar.

They would soon need rescuing themselves, he thought.

His master would be pleased.

CHAPTER SEVEN

"You sure about this?" Cabe asked, cringing when he realized what he'd done.

Taj stiffened and snarled at him. "You know I hate that question."

"It makes it no less valid, though," Lina commented. "You're taking an awful chance doing this."

"Which is why I'm doing it, no one else," she answered.

"That still doesn't answer my question," Cabe told her.

She turned and pecked him on the lips.

"And kissing up on me isn't gonna distract me either," he said.

Torbon raised his hand. "It would me," he called out. "I'm next."

Lina elbowed him in the ribs, doubling him over with a, "Whoof!"

"No one is next," the engineer declared, "especially not you."

Krawg brushed the fur out of his face and puckered up.

"You sure? I could be convinced to keep these ruffians in line for a kiss."

Taj rolled her eyes. "Yes, gack it, I'm sure," she answered, jabbing a finger Krawg's direction to make sure he knew she was talking to him. "I'm not kissing anyone else, and I'm going. It's decided."

"But we don't know when Commander Rolkar or whoever will come back to collect us," Cabe argued. "It could be any minute now."

"Then I'm wasting time sitting here arguing with you," she replied.

Her clothes wavered and shifted from the fancy royal garb she'd been wearing into a tight black suit that emphasized her lean build. The material shimmered as it absorbed the light in the room.

"I still don't think you should do it," Cabe argued, "but I definitely don't think you should do it alone. Let me come with you."

"We should all go," Torbon said.

"Then what happens when no one is here to meet with the queen?" Lina asked. "You think they're gonna just let that go without looking into it?" She sighed, shaking her head. "We came here with a cover, and we need to maintain it." Lina pointed at Taj. "I don't necessarily agree with her idea, but with us being locked down in the palace thanks to that clustergack that happened on our way here, I'm not thinking we have much of a choice."

"While I also agree it's not the wisest course of action given that we have no definitive time frame for our meeting with Queen Rilan," Dent told the crew, "I'm also seeing little option here if we are to find Grom Hadar in a timely manner. *Someone* must go out and search for him."

"Why can't that someone be you?" Cabe asked Dent, clearly frustrated by his inability to convince Taj not to run off and do something stupid.

"Because he's our representative," Taj explained. "He'll be the one speaking for us, he's the one who has all the answers, and he's the one who can convince the queen that we might actually have something they want from us."

"And you think they won't notice you missing?" Cabe went on, unwilling to let it go.

"I'm sick," Taj replied with a cough, holding her stomach. "The journey and the stress of the attack made me ill," she explained with a sly grin. "We're supposed to be these pampered little royals, so they'll believe that, but not if all of us are gone and there's only Dent and Krawg here."

"If all of you are going, then so am I," Krawg complained. He glanced at the serving carts, which he and Torbon had visited many times since they'd been brought in. "Besides, you need someone to carry the food."

"I like the way you think, Krawg," Torbon told the Ursite, wandering over to the carts again and grabbing a meat wrap for himself and one for Krawg, tossing it to the Ursite. Krawg grunted and stuffed the wrap in his mouth.

"No one else is going!" Taj nearly shouted, raising her hands in frustration when she realized how loud she'd gotten. "Just me, and I'm going now," she said, backing away from the group and marching toward the rear bedroom where they'd located a window that led out of the palace and toward the town. She paused at the door and glanced over her shoulder at the crew. "Cover for me when they come to collect us. I won't be gone long."

"We'll stay in touch on the comm," Dent told her, "but be cautious out there. If we are to remain in the role of a royal Furlorian attaché, then you might well and truly be on your own once you leave the palace. It's likely we won't be able to rush off and come after you should something occur."

Taj nodded.

"Be careful," Cabe muttered, turning to join Torbon and Krawg at the cart, finally surrendering to the idea of Taj going off on her own.

There wasn't time to argue with him anymore. The longer Grom was out there, the more likely something bad could occur.

She couldn't let that happen.

She went to the window and eased it open. Lina had already checked it and disabled the alarm systems so the Orgesse people wouldn't know she'd used it to get out of the palace. Lina had also used her suit's systems to subtly move the security cameras aimed at the rooms so it gave Taj a straight shot down into the palace grounds and a delineated path to follow that would get her out of the grounds and away without being noticed by the automated security systems.

All she had to worry about were the guards patrolling the physical property down below.

Fortunately, her suit could handle that.

She covered her head completely, then triggered the chameleon mode of her armored suit. She immediately blended in with her surroundings, her clothing mimicking the shadows and the gray of the palace walls.

With the help of the suit's servos, she sunk her claws into the wall and scrambled downward as fast as she could, only the barest of *tinks* sounding at her efforts. She made it to the ground in moments, and shot off behind nearby foliage. Her suit compensated and shifted to its new camo seamlessly.

She stopped to catch her breath as proximity sensors flashed on her eyepiece, letting her know a pair of guards were passing. Taj heard them chatting with one another and traced their steps until they disappeared from her screen. Then she bolted off across the yard, following the path highlighted by her suit's systems.

She grinned as she ran.

This thing is amazing, she thought over the link to Dent.

Just don't get too comfortable, the AI replied. *Rely on it too much and you'll get lazy and make a mistake. It's a tool, nothing more, remember that. Stick to your training and instincts.*

Way to kill the thrill, Dent, she thought back, but she knew he was right.

She focused on the task at hand and clambered up the wall that bordered the palace and let out into the city beyond. This part, she knew, would be the most difficult of her escape.

The security systems there were better overlapped and designed to keep people out—and, unfortunately, in. It was also made redundant and more difficult by the increase of physical personnel patrolling both the top and other side of the wall.

Taj crouched low in the shadows by the wall and

reached a hand out, avoiding actually touching it, however. Her palm hovered centimeters from the wall.

I'm here, she sent to Lina.

On it, the engineer replied without hesitation.

Taj watched her display flicker and saw the various processes run across the screen that Lina was using to manipulate the security protocols built into the wall. Seconds seemed to drag out forever before Lina finally said the process was over.

Got it done, she thought. *The systems will now process your suit as part of it. Just be sure to keep completely covered or you risk setting it off.*

Taj shot up the wall without waiting, trusting the engineer to have done what she said. She climbed quickly, like a spider, keeping her chest and stomach right up against the wall.

She was about halfway up when a motion detector warned her someone was standing overhead.

Taj froze, clutching to the wall as she spied a pale face peek over the edge of the wall from above.

"What is it?" someone out of sight asked.

"Thought I heard something," the guard peering over the wall said. He stared directly at her.

Taj held her breath, even though she was sure the man couldn't possibly hear the whisper that was her breath through the layers of the suit. Still, she couldn't help herself.

Like Dent had said earlier, she had to go with her instincts and not trust the AI's technology more than necessary.

She hung there in frigid silence as the guard continued

to look, squinting as he tried to the locate the source of whatever he'd heard. After a long moment, the guard shrugged and his face moved out of sight.

Taj let out the barest of sighs.

"I'm not seeing anything," the guard said to his compatriot.

"You know how sound carries weirdly from the palace," his partner said. "Besides, the systems would have been triggered if there was something there. No one gets over the wall," the second guard told the first, absolute confidence in his voice.

"True," the first replied, and Taj heard their booted footsteps as they moved on.

She watched on her scanner until they were gone, then started her ascent again. Seconds later, she was on the top of the wall. She cast a furtive glance at the area beyond, letting her suit scan for more guards and the best route, then she leapt into the air.

Taj soared out over the external security barriers and landed in a crouch. She rolled, letting her momentum carry her even farther from the guards and their sensors, and then hunkered down low and bolted toward the nearest cover of town.

In an alley a short distance away from the wall, out of the line of sight of anyone manning it, she straightened, stretching her hunched limbs, and grinned. There was no hint that she'd triggered the alarms crossing the wall.

I'm out, she told her crew.

Systems look good, Lina confirmed.

Talk soon, Taj shot back, knowing how little time they had. The clock was ticking.

Be careful, she heard Cabe say again, and the system went silent.

I will, she thought to herself, not risking sending another message.

The original plan had been to simply transform her suit into a reasonable approximation of the local fashion and walk down the streets boldly in her quest to find Grom Hadar, but the attack and news footage gacked that all up.

Taj, keeping her suit fully sealed and the chameleon program running, climbed up the side of the building she'd been resting against and clambered onto the roof. She immediately scanned the area, searching for people she might not be able to see, and she was glad to find herself alone.

Not much choice but to trust in the tech out here, she thought.

Regardless, she would do what she needed to do.

Taj started off, skirting the rooftops and leaping from building to building as she made her way toward Grom's last-known location.

The Federation intel had tracked Grom's last transmission to them and had provided Taj's team with the location. It was apparently a small building near the edge of town, hidden away in an area Dent had unkindly called a ghetto.

Though Taj hadn't heard the word before, Dent's explanation was spot on once she'd traversed the city and found her way to the coordinates displayed on her screen.

The place looked like a warzone.

Much like where the caravan had been ambushed, this part of town was in poor repair and crowded with trash and people who looked like refugees. Taj felt sorry for them immediately as she looked upon the people wandering the streets, seemingly with nowhere to go. They were dressed in layers of clothing despite the obvious warmth of the night, and they carried handfuls of ragged bags slung over their shoulders and in their hands.

It was like they carted along everything they owned for fear of leaving it someplace and losing it.

She felt a pang in her chest at the thought, the feeling further motivated by just how many people were out at that time of night. While not overly late, the local businesses and traffic had closed and cleared out, but Taj could count at least twenty people shuffling along.

They kept their distance from one another, and she saw wary looks pass between a few as they drew too close, each of the people shuffling off to regain that separation without so much as a word.

She couldn't imagine living like that. Even the few people she disliked among the Furlorians had never provoked such a response from her, even on their worst days. Taj wondered what it was like to be so harangued in her daily life that she needed to avoid those of the same circumstances living around her.

That was probably the desperation and despair that had Grom seeking out the Federation.

Reminded of her mission, Taj waited until the streets were partially clear before clambering down the wall into a darkened alley that sensors marked as empty. She slipped behind the backs of the shuffling locals and darted across the street into an adjoining alleyway between two short, squat buildings.

Both were rundown and battered, many of the windows haphazardly boarded shut, while pieces of the boards had been cracked or ripped away. She made her way down the alley, searching for the specific location as her sensors ticked off coordinates. At last, she found the hovel where Grom had last reached out to the Federation.

After a quick glance about, making certain she wasn't seen despite the scanner's clear readings, Taj grabbed the door handle and tugged.

Despite appearances, the door seemingly nailed to the wall, it gave way easily, opening with a mournful *creak*. Taj hissed at the sound and shot inside, easing the door closed behind her and hoping the sound didn't carry.

As she waited to see if anyone noticed, she spied a pair of thick bolts that had been installed on the inside of the door. She slipped them into place and felt slightly better about her position.

No obvious signs of damage to those bolts. If this was Grom's hideout, it would appear that he'd left of his own accord, not that he'd been forced out, which seemed to be a good thing.

Taj hoped that meant his belongings would still be there, at the very least, and maybe she could find something that might lead her to where he'd gone.

She drew in a deep breath and started her search of the makeshift home. It was small, dank, and sparse. The foyer she entered was tiny, barely enough room for her to stand there alone. There was no way two people would fit in it side by side.

Beyond that, there was a cramped kitchen, though she was only able to tell that by the counters that filled the room. There weren't any conveniences, nothing for heating or cooling food, but a single plate setting with utensils sat on one of the counters alongside a small sink. It looked clean, and Taj couldn't smell any food remnants.

In fact, she could smell nothing but dust through the suit's filters.

She moved on past the empty kitchen and found a singular main room, designed to be the whole of the apartment, both bedroom and living area, with only a bathroom off to the side through an open alcove. Taj could tell it was empty from where she stood without needing to go over to it.

She glanced around the room and let out a slow sigh. The place was only marginally better than living on the streets, she imagined.

At least it would keep the rain off your head, she thought, glancing up at the ceiling. *Then again...*

The ceiling had a number of darker spots across its face, showing where past rains or leaks had infiltrated the room. Bits of plaster and wood hung from the ceiling like thick spider webs.

Taj peeled her eyes from the ceiling and turned to where a small couch sat shoved into the corner. A pillow and a pair of ratty blankets were tossed on top, the blankets crumpled into a bunch near the foot.

The floor creaked as Taj went to take a closer look, letting the suit's scanners ensure her safe passage.

Next to the couch, she spotted a small pack. She snatched it up and looked inside.

There were mostly dirty outfits wadded inside, an extra pair of tattered shoes, and a few protein bars, once of which was half-eaten and left open. But as Taj dug around inside the bag, she found a clasped envelope, stuffed nearly to bursting.

She pulled the envelope out and opened it.

Inside were a thick stack of images, one after another. They weren't anything like the holos she'd seen growing up on Krawlas, where the device flowed through the images, displaying each in turn in 3-D. No, each of these images were singular, one moment captured on each picture, though it did appear as if they were intended to be a series.

As she flipped through the images, there were slight movements by the subjects in each, allowing her to get an idea as to the motion being performed by those movements the images captured. And while several people flitted across the pictures, it looked as if Grom had singled out one among the gathering.

The man stood with obvious confidence among the group, set apart in the center of them. The room was gloomy and candlelit, casting shadowy wisps across the scene, but there was something ritualistic about the setting that caught Taj's attention.

There were strange symbols painted in white on the floor and walls that Taj didn't recognize and her suit's system didn't seem capable of translating. The man held a book aloft, its cover at a bad angle where Taj couldn't even attempt to identify it, but he seemed to be waving it about, motioning with it toward those gathered around him. The way it was used in the images, held out before everyone, made her think it was important.

Like the man in the center of the photo, those around him were also dressed in black robes. Each of them wore a similarly dark, hooded mask that obscured their features when they were captured in the images. The fact that there were slits for four eyes on each of the masks told Taj that those hiding underneath were most likely locals.

It also told her that they were most likely the same group of people who'd attacked the caravan since they were wearing the same type of masks.

The man in the center of the images wore a hood similar to those of the crowd, but it was designed more like a hat. His face stood out pale against the darkness of his clothing and the shadowy room. His four eyes were narrow slits of yellow, and his mouth peeled back in a sneer in most every picture, his cheeks and forehead lined with intensity.

Whatever he was saying to the people there, he meant it. There was clear determination in his expression, a fire that stood out plainly.

As Taj flipped through the images and landed on the last one, she caught sight of the man's eyes. Unlike before, when he'd been focused on his flock—as Taj couldn't help but picture him as a shepherd—his eyes now looked directly at her. She felt a sudden rush of adrenaline as if the man could see her. A chill ran down her spine at the intensity of his glare.

His arm had begun to rise in the picture, as if moving to point, and the determination in the man's expression had been replaced by something more calculated, something more sinister.

Fury.

Taj realized then that the man had noticed whoever was taking the images—Grom, she presumed—and had reacted to his unexpected presence. He'd spotted Grom, which was what she figured had been the cause of the crew's mission there. This was why he disappeared.

Obviously, however, for her to have the images in her hands right then, Grom had gotten away from the group.

For a time, at least.

The thought sobered Taj as she realized these people in the images might well be the reason Grom disappeared. She had no idea what information he had intended to provide the Federation in exchange for protection.

We have a problem, Lina thought over the link. *They're here to get us.*

Taj growled and stuffed the images back into the envelope. Once she was done, she pressed the whole thing to her chest and willed the suit to absorb it, marveling at the process as it did just that, drawing the envelope into the mass of the suit and leaving no trace of it once it was gone.

They're asking for you, Lina went on.

"Cover for me for a few minutes," she said, not even realizing she'd spoken aloud. "I'm on my way."

Taj spun on her heel and bolted back for the door. She scanned outside and, when she was sure she could slip out unseen, she threw the bolts back and took off, racing back toward the palace as fast as she possibly could.

She hoped she'd make it back in time.

CHAPTER EIGHT

"I'm so sorry young Princess Taj fell ill," Dent explained to Zel as he led them through the palace, presumably toward where the queen awaited them.

"Queen Rilan will be greatly disappointed," Zel said. Krawg grunted, as if taking offense at the rep's tone of voice.

Lina certainly had.

"I understand," Lina said, jumping in and cutting off Dent before he could say anything else, "but she's not used to being ambushed and shot at, forced to use a weapon directly to defend herself. The whole situation simply overwhelmed her. To be completely honest, I'm surprised the rest of us are doing as well as we are. We could all use a short rest."

Zel nibbled at his lip, and Lina realized it was an effort by the man to keep his own frustration in check. "Of course, of course," he replied, but the engineer didn't see much in the way of real understanding there.

His only interest was in satisfying his queen, and the circumstances of what had happened to the crew didn't matter except in the regards that it had inconvenienced his monarch, thus it had inconvenienced him.

That was all he cared about, Lina thought.

She, however, had another concern.

Lina slowed and leaned against the wall, exhaling loudly. The crew stopped and gathered around her.

"Are you okay?" Torbon asked, concern in his eyes. If she hadn't been so intent on playing the role, she would have laughed at him.

I'm fine, she thought across the link. *Play along.*

"A little lightheaded is all," Lina said out loud, making sure that Zel heard her.

"Here, lean against me," Cabe told her, wrapping an arm around her waist when Torbon just stood there, obviously trying to catch up on everything.

Slick, Cabe teased, and Torbon offered a tiny shrug in an attempt at defense.

"Are you well?" Zel asked, coming to stand behind the mass of Furlorians as they tended to Lina.

Krawg stepped forward, forcing the representative back a step.

"She'll be fine," Dent answered for Lina, also coming to stand before Zel, helping to obscure his view a bit. "She just needs a moment or two to recover."

"If there's anything—" Zel started, but Dent waved the offer off before the rep could finish it.

"No need," Dent said, shaking his head. "I assure you, she'll be fine."

Zel nodded. "Good to hear, of course, but Queen Rilan

awaits us." He glanced around the room carefully, then eased in close to Dent. "I'm afraid her majesty is not the most patient of monarchs, if you understand my point. I think it best we move on," he said. "It is enough that we are missing one of your entourage, but to be late might well stress her majesty unduly."

Lina heard the implied threat in Zel's voice. She could see their cover being blown shortly if the queen lost her patience with the Furlorians. Given the ambush, Lina could already imagine the queen was furious at how things had transpired with the trade delegation. The visit, which had been a last minute one arranged by the Federation, was likely already a bit of an annoyance to the queen, but to pile more difficulties on top of it would strain the most patient of hosts, which the queen was not.

Zel's words made her think it wouldn't be good.

"I'm fine now," Lina said, straightening and shaking off Cabe and stepping out of their protective circle. "We've no desire to offend the queen or disrespect her hospitality."

A relieved grin spread across Zel's face. He made a shallow bow to Lina. "Thank you for understanding," he told her and spun about, waving them on. "Please come, the queen awaits."

If you're coming, you need to hurry, Lina sent to Taj.

The engineer bit back a groan after a moment when Taj didn't respond, so she marched on behind the nervously chattering representative as he led them toward the throne room. A short while later, a giant pair of etched doors appeared at the end of the hall, looming before them.

The rep held up a hand for the crew to stop, and he turned to face them. "Please, wait here while I introduce you. I'll then return to lead you inside," he told them. "Please, remember to honor Queen Rilan as you stand before her."

Zel turned away without waiting for an answer and marched to the doors. One side crept open, a guard holding it, and he slipped inside, the door closing behind him.

Lina let out a sigh, staring after the rep despite not being able to see him.

"What do we do?" Torbon whispered.

"What we came here to do," Lina replied. "Sell the idea that we're here to trade with the Zoranthians, nothing more." She motioned to Dent. "Let him lead the way and don't say anything...*anything*," she emphasized, "unless you are spoken to directly, understood?"

"You act like I'm gonna screw things up," he said, pouting.

"Probably because you will," Cabe confirmed, patting him on the shoulder.

Torbon huffed and glanced at Krawg then Dent. Both raised an eyebrow and nodded their agreement.

"Fine," Torbon whined. "I'll keep my mouth shut."

Right then, one of the grand doors opened again, this time much wider, showing off part of the throne room past the Heltrol soldier who stood guard. Zel waved them forward.

Gack it, Taj, Lina cursed over the link. *It's too late.*

There was a shuffle of footsteps behind them, and Lina saw Zel's eyes brighten just before she spun about, catching sight of Taj, her suit once more shifted into the outfit she'd worn initially.

Never too late, Taj said over the link, offering a grin Lina's direction.

"My apologies, Zel," she said as she strode up to join the rest of the crew. "The flux passed quickly, and I felt it best to join my siblings as they meet the queen."

Zel let out a relieved sigh he clearly thought no one heard, and he smiled broadly. "So glad you could join us," he said, bowing to Taj. "No need to apologize. Your timing is impeccable."

You hear that? Taj asked over the mental link. *Impeccable.*

If you say so, Lina replied, fighting back the urge to snarl at her friend.

Cabe came over beside her and bumped her gently, slipping her a sideways smile. *You find anything?*

I'll report in a bit, she answered, quickly moving forward to be behind Zel as he entered the throne room and announced them in person this time. *Stay on task for now,* she ordered.

See? Torbon sent, shaking his head. *No fun at all.*

Lina eased between Torbon and Taj to keep anything from happening, and the crew made their way into the throne room.

The sheer size of it took their breath away.

Great wooden rafters supported the sloped ceiling, looking as if they crisscrossed the sky. A blood red carpet ran the length of the room, slipping serpentine up the steps of the great dais at the far end of the room.

Lina had expected there to be an audience in the vast room, but the only people present besides the crew and Zel were the queen herself, upon her throne, the guards, and a woman Lina hadn't seen before.

Commander Rolkar stood at attention near the first step of the dais, and her Heltrol soldiers lined the room along the sides, standing on a high ledge that ran the length of the floor. Columned alcoves loomed behind the soldiers, forming a space where Lina believed most of the visitors would be made to stand, were there any.

The Orgesse banner hung on the wall behind the throne, its red and black standing out in sharp contrast to the gray of the stone room.

"This way," Zel urged, waving them on as casually as the man could. His head was slumped, as if he didn't dare look directly at his monarch.

Follow his lead, Taj warned, knowing they needed to get this right for Grom's sake.

The crew murmured their agreement over the link and formed up, doing their best to appear regal. Except for Krawg, who, no matter how hard he tried, could only look furry.

Lina would have laughed at everyone's effort if she hadn't noticed that she, too, was walking straighter and more rigid, carrying herself as though she were made of glass.

"Your Majesty," Zel began, bowing so deeply Lina feared the man might topple over. He didn't, to her surprise, and he straightened once Queen Rilan acknowledged him with a nod. "I present to you your Furlorian guests, the princes and princesses Merr."

Lina swallowed hard at hearing Mama's name attached to them. Even though she'd known it was coming, the plan laid out ahead of time, memories of the old queen flooded back right then. She sniffed quietly, covering her moistening eyes behind the bow that everyone began around her.

By the time she'd lifted her head, she had herself back under control.

"Greetings, Furlorians," the queen said, offering them a practiced smile.

The crew returned the greetings as they'd practiced, letting Taj and Dent lead the way while they kept quiet.

"Greetings, your majesty," Taj replied. "It is our pleasure to be granted an opportunity to speak with you, especially given such short notice."

While Taj spoke, Lina examined the queen.

While she had the same four eyes as her people, it was clear the queen was a better genetic specimen than most of those they'd seen so far.

Her face was lean and perfectly even, the button of her nose set in the center of her face above full lips that sat pursed when she wasn't speaking. Long, white hair flowed smoothly back from her scalp, where it hung over her shoulders like fine wire, not the slightest crimp or imperfection present.

Queen Rilan sat straight on her throne, but she didn't look stiff. She simply looked regal, much the way the crew could only pretend to be. Her small, manicured hands were crossed in her lap, set so delicately on the fabric of her dress that Lina could not see a single wrinkle formed by their presence.

The woman stared out at the crew with all four eyes gleaming, and Lina spied a glimmer behind the look that spoke of intelligence and calculation. The queen wasn't simply greeting them, readying for their pitch, she was evaluating them, taking their measure.

Lina stiffened at the realization as Taj went on, selling the queen on the basic gist of why they'd come to the planet to begin with.

"And this...Toradium-42, as you call it, has sufficient energy to power the whole of my country with only a small amount?"

"And then some, Your Majesty," Dent answered, slipping in to better cover the technical aspects of the mineral. "It dwarfs any of the energy sources you currently have available to you, and it would be the catalyst to an age of advancement never before seen upon Zoranthan."

Don't oversell it, Dent, Taj said over the link, her frustration clear.

Only doing what is necessary to achieve our goal, Dent replied, continuing his discussion with the queen.

Queen Rilan seemed to stiffen at hearing Dent's proclamation. She leaned forward so slightly that Lina thought she'd imagined it at first. "And this mineral...it has uses other than simply harnessing energy for fuel?"

The unspoken question hung heavily in the air.

Dent nodded. "Yes, Your Majesty. Toradium-42 can be used both to power your local energy needs but also those of your spacecraft and your defensive needs."

Lina rolled her eyes at the AI's subtlety, framing the answer in a defensive manner rather than making it clear the Toradium-42 could be used to power massive weapons on top of everything else.

Queen Rilan smiled gently, though Lina could see the predatory nature of it, and eased back in her seat.

"The mineral is quite stable in its base form, too," Dent went on, "and is easily transported without any but the most basic of safety precautions. It's also undetectable by most energy scanners, its nature unknown across the universe except to those, like you, wise enough to understand its effectiveness."

Wow! Torbon said. *I want to buy some, too. What a pitch.*

Taj snuck a furtive glare Torbon's direction, and Lina thumped her foot with his, shutting him up before he could say anything else.

Dent eased forward and pulled out a sample of the Toradium-42. Commander Rolkar came over and plucked it out of Dent's hand as if it might explode.

Lina stared at the shiny mineral in the vial, it reminding her of her home and the cruel attack of the Wyyvans in their effort to claim it. She wondered how badly the lizard-like aliens had ruined the planet since they'd taken over.

"We brought a small sample for your technicians to test and experiment with, but it will most certainly be enough for you to see its effectiveness, given its power." Dent smiled at the queen. "We look forward to hearing your thoughts once they've been given time to examine the Toradium-42."

"As I look forward to discussing terms once my scientists have evaluated the mineral," the queen answered, still smiling.

Lina could see the thoughts swirling in the woman's head as if her skull were a fish bowl. No matter what happened, there was no way the Furlorians could allow the queen to get her hands on a real source of Toradium-42. The small sample they'd found among Captain Vort's things after he'd been killed was scary enough. Lina hoped the queen and her scientists weren't able to recreate the mineral.

Dent's earlier assurances that she couldn't replicate it didn't feel as reassuring now as she watched the queen stare at the mineral in Rolkar's hands.

"Thank you for both your time and your hospitality, Your Majesty," Dent finished, cluing the Furlorians in that it was time to bow again.

They did, and the queen said her farewells, Zel leading the crew from the throne room and back out through the great double-doors. He escorted them to their chambers, and Lina watched as Taj snarled when the bolts were drawn outside once again, the array of Heltrol soldiers still out there.

Lina held up a hand and called for silence until she and Dent scanned the room and their surroundings once more. After they finished, they motioned that everything was okay.

"You think she believed us?" Cabe asked with a huff, looking as if he'd held his breath the entire time they'd been scanning.

Lina nodded. "I do. Did you see that look she gave the Toradium when Dent handed it over? She looked like she was ready to devour it whole, she wanted it so badly."

Dent agreed. "My analysis of her reaction is quite similar, albeit more technical," he said with a sly smile. "She most certainly wants the Toradium-42 to be real and available to her as soon as possible. She has plans for it, clearly."

"It's so she can blow the gack out of her enemies,

nothing more," Taj grunted, shaking her head and baring her teeth.

"Who cares what she wants it for?" Cabe retorted. "It's not like she's gonna get more than that tiny vial anyway. She doesn't know where Krawlas is, and she sure as gack doesn't know that there's an army of Wyyvan sitting there more than happy to shoot her out of the sky if she does find out."

Lina sighed. "Still, the look on her face... Wow. It was terrifying. I'd hate to be on her bad side."

"Which is why we need to complete our mission and get out of here before things fall apart any more than they already have," Torbon said, turning to Taj. "You find anything interesting?"

"I did indeed." She nodded and willed her suit to spit out the images. She spread them out on the table before the crew.

"What are these?" Cabe asked, examining the pictures.

"Photographs," Dent answered. "An old-fashioned method of capturing images in a single frame rather than on a holographic device." He glanced over at Taj. "Where did you find these?"

"They were in Grom's place," she answered. "He wasn't, though."

Dent flipped through the mass of images and nodded. "Given the nature of the last frame, I suspect this series of photographs is exactly why he wasn't there."

"Most likely. I had the same feeling," Taj said. "His place was empty, but it didn't look as if anyone had been there, so he had to have gotten away from these guys," she announced, gesturing to the stack of images. "His disappearance happened after he'd made it home and gone back out."

"It still stands to reason that his sudden vanishing act was inspired by these photos, given how they appear," Dent argued, tapping the man in the hat on one of the photos. "As such, it seems our next best chance of seeking out Grom Hadar is by finding this man here. He might not be the cause of Grom vanishing, but it certainly looks as though he's involved."

"Can you scan these images and do a search of the local news and database archives?" Taj asked.

Dent nodded. "I can, but it won't be quick, and the quality is going to be an issue given the primitive nature of these images."

Taj sighed. "Well, it's not like we have a whole lot of options, Dent," she told the AI. "Grom's room was empty of leads other than these photos, and unless we run around asking the neighbors if they saw anything, we're already butting our head against a wall."

"They'd probably recognize us from the news anyway," Cabe complained.

"I'm not sure they would, at least not out there," Taj countered. "The folks living around Grom's hideout are mostly vagrants, people living on the street. I'm not sure they have access to the news easily or if they'd even care if they did."

"Probably best we don't push our luck and risk it unless we have to," Dent said. "Let me try this first, then we'll see what other options there are left to us should this not work."

Taj agreed and let out a yawn, muffling it with her

hand. "I think that's our best bet for now. If we go out without a location in mind and just wander about, we'll likely run into trouble."

It had been a long day of travel, and the excitement of the trip and the ambush and Taj's stealthy trip to Grom's home had sapped the energy from her. She started off toward the room she and Cabe had claimed after their arrival.

"I need to rest for a bit," she told them. "Keep an eye on the door while you're processing those images, Dent, and wake me up as soon as you figure anything out, no matter how minor."

"Will do, Captain," Dent told her, grinning as he began to work on the images, using his eyes to scan them into the memory of his android body so he could process them in turn.

Taj groaned and crept off, Cabe following. As much as she'd wanted to rush out into the city to find Grom, her little foray earlier had made it clear that he wasn't going to be found as easily as she'd hoped. They were looking at a marathon, not a sprint. As such, Taj needed to get some sleep.

She wanted to be sharp for whatever stood in their way.

Taj had a feeling it would only get harder from there.

CHAPTER NINE

The massive crash of shattering glass pulled Taj from deep sleep.

She bolted upright, Cabe doing the same beside her. Both stared at each other for a moment, thoughts whirling as they fought to shake off sleep and determine what was going on.

We're under attack! Dent screamed over the link, confirming the worst.

Taj rolled off the side of the bed and triggered her suit, which she'd worn to bed in the form of a pair of soft, silk pajamas. Her armor took shape, covering her from head to toe as she stormed out of the room. Cabe did the same behind her, albeit a little bit slower.

He was always slow to wake up.

Krawg clearly wasn't.

Taj stepped out of the room just as the giant Ursite went flying past her. He slammed into the wall near the front door with a loud grunt, then toppled to his butt to stare furiously across the room. Taj followed his glare, and her breath caught in her lungs for an instant as she froze.

A battle droid nearly the same size as the Ursite hovered in the middle of the room. Eight arms jutted from the armored torso of the bot, four of them ending in clamping metal claws, the others in wide hammers that looked like makeshift fists. One of those had been what struck Krawg.

Cabe bumped into her back at her unexpected pause, then managed to squeeze past her into the room, still not entirely awake yet.

"Oh...gack," he said, clearly regretting his choice to step out of the room and into the line of robotic aggression.

The droid shot straight toward the pair, and a long metal arm clasped Cabe's biceps and swung him about before he could react. Taj growled as Cabe was whipped around in a circle and slammed into the nearby wall. Plaster and wood exploded in his wake, showering Taj and kicking up a wake of powdery dust.

The bot reversed its arm and flung Cabe across the room, where he smashed into the array of food carts still out from the night before. Food and drinks and limbs went flying in a messy tangle.

"Cabe!" Taj shouted, leaping at the bot with feral intent.

"I'm fine," he answered across the comm. "Suit absorbed the worst of it," Cabe clarified, "but I wouldn't—"

He didn't get the rest out before Taj collided with the battle droid.

"—get too close to it," he finished with a sigh.

She managed to strike a blow against its armor before one of the clawed hands, much faster than she could have imagined, snatched her off its robotic frame. Then one of the fists slammed into her ribs. Her breath spewed from her lungs, and the droid hit her again before she had a chance to react.

The fist pistoned into her side, once, twice, and made ready for a third.

Taj saw a blur of movement behind the droid, recognizing it as Dent, but she knew she couldn't rely on him, or anyone, to save her. She had to do it herself.

So she did.

She swung her legs up and drove them hard into the battle droid's torso, much like it had done to her with its fist. Taj powered up her kick right before she blasted it, her booted feet slamming into the metal hull with a resounding *clank!* The bot shot backward in the air.

"Heads up," she called as she broke free of the droid's grasp, realizing Dent was awful close to where she'd kicked the bot, but she didn't need to worry.

Dent sidestepped the flying droid and added to its momentum with a blow of his own, driving the bot into the wall near where Krawg had landed earlier. The Ursite, having cleared the area just in time, stared as the droid crashed through the wall beside him and out into the hallway beyond.

That was when Taj realized it wasn't alone.

"Bloody Rowl!" she cried out, staring at the carnage in the corridor.

Where the cluster of Heltrol guards had been stationed was now a bloody mess. The second droid was better armed and clearly deadlier. Where the first had metallic fists, the second had sharpened blades that vibrated with vicious brutality. In its clawed hands, the droid held pieces of soldiers that had been hacked away from their owners, showers of blood being flung everywhere.

"We have a problem," Lina called out, catching sight of the second battle droid. "There's another one."

"No gack!" Taj replied as the first droid spun about and pushed its way back into the room, while the second continued its murder spree of the guards.

A burst of weapon fire caught it coming in, but it did little more than slow its advance. Black scorch marks welled up on its armored hull, though they didn't seem to do more than cosmetic damage.

"That's not good," Lina muttered, hitting the trigger again to blast the bot once more. Bursts of energy struck it again, but the bot twisted in the air, causing the bolts to careen harmlessly off its frame, and it shot forward.

Krawg caught it before it got far.

The Ursite grabbed one of the bot's arms and redirected it downward, driving it into the floor with a loud *thud*. He kicked it for good measure and yanked hard on the mechanical arm as the droid shot away from him.

There was a painful screech of metal scraping against metal, and Krawg came away with one of the robot's arms in his hands. He waved it in the air triumphantly and roared.

The droid bounced off the wall and came away in a frenzied burst of motion. It whipped itself in a circle, spinning like a top. Its arms whirled around like shrieking blades, heading straight toward Krawg. The Ursite willed his weapon out of his suit, but Taj could tell he wouldn't get it out and up in time.

Fortunately, Torbon landed a flying kick on the side of the battle droid's head where there weren't any swinging arms.

Torbon bounced away, clawing at the ceiling to control his landing, and the droid toppled sideways. Its arms struck the ground, tearing at the plush carpet, and the impact whipped it about unexpectedly.

Two more of its arms went flying as the droid crashed into the ground, its momentum yanking it suddenly sideways. It slammed into the nearby wall, and Cabe unloaded a barrage of fire into its smoking frame.

"Aim for the joints where the arms were torn out," Taj called, doing exactly that herself.

Her first two shots struck the hull as the battle droid continued to move, trying to right itself, but her third shot hit the target dead on, slipping past the armor and doing some real damage.

Sparks hissed and flew from the joint, followed by black smoke, but the clean shot hadn't stopped it.

It righted itself with the remaining arms and spun about, flying straight toward Taj.

"Looks like you pissed it off," Torbon told her, running up alongside the battle droid.

"Yeah," Taj replied, staring as the droid came at her.

Again though, Torbon inserted himself into the fight. He triggered the energy blade on his right arm and drove the sword into another of the robot's open joints. Sparks flew again, and Torbon pushed hard, amplifying his strength with the suit's resources.

The blade pierced the droid's insides, and Torbon twisted his wrist upwards, letting the blade cleave through the bot's electronics as it angled towards its head. Then as the droid twisted sideways to shake him free and minimize the damage, Torbon retracted his blade and leapt away.

The bot smoked and squeed as it spun about, twitching spasmodically. It didn't have time to react beyond that as Dent stepped directly up to it and unloaded his weapon into a narrow slit where Torbon's blade had pierced the armor from its inside.

The droid's head spat sparks and went still.

A second later, the bot whistled and fell to its side, landing with a loud *crash*.

"Excellent work," Cabe congratulated, but Taj knew the fight wasn't over yet.

"Stay alert," she warned, and sure enough, the second battle droid, apparently sensing the defeat of its partner, burst through the wall beside the door.

Its vibrating blades spattered blood across the room.

"This one's pissed," Torbon said, triggering his blades once more and dropping into a defensive position.

"If I were to guess," Dent started, "I'd say the first of the droids was attempting to capture, not kill, us. This one, however..."

"Clearly has no such compunctions," Lina finished for the AI.

"Wonderful," Cabe muttered, raising his gun and unleashing a burst of fire before the battle droid engaged. "But there's no point waiting on it to kill us," he said. "Hit it."

Bursts of energy bounced off its armored hull, doing little more than scorching the metal. It advanced with a purpose, swinging its blades at Cabe in vicious arcs. Cabe sidestepped the first two attacks but was caught by the third.

The blade sliced at him, but his armor held, stiffening in response to the attack and deflecting it, albeit barely.

Cabe stumbled back with a shout, holding his forearm.

Taj engaged the droid from the side to draw its focus, and Lina joined her. Both Furlorians hit the trigger on their weapons as fast as they could, slamming the battle droid with a barrage of fire.

But unlike the other one, which had been damaged and provided access to its internals, this one barely reacted to the onslaught. It shot forward, spinning to minimize the damage from the blasts, and flew straight toward Taj and Lina, weapons flailing.

It never reached them.

A hunk of metal flew over their heads and slammed into the streaking droid with a massive clang that made everyone's ears ring. Taj ducked and blinked in amazement as she watched Krawg use the fallen droid as a battering ram against its companion.

The functioning droid was knocked backwards, spinning in circles, but the crew didn't let up.

Torbon slashed at it with his own blades, cleaving two of its arms off at the shoulders. Cabe slunk low and stepped around Torbon immediately after his attack and blasted the droid over and over up close and personal, emptying his weapon.

When Cabe willed an extra magazine out of his armor, Dent attacked.

He drove his android fist into the head of the battle droid, sending it into the wall with a crash. As it bounced back, Dent stepped to the side and struck it in the back of its head, knocking it to the floor.

The battle droid kicked and shrieked and made to rise, but Krawg had figured out the best way to take it down.

The Ursite stood above the fallen droid, its deactivated partner held over his head. He brought the other droid down on top of the still-functioning one. The room echoed with the metallic *clang* of their impact, shaking the floor beneath the crew's feet.

But Krawg hadn't finished.

He lifted the broken droid again and again, slamming it down on the other until both were nothing more than twisted heaps of metal. At last, when the second bot stopped moving, Krawg grunted and tossed his makeshift weapon aside, clearly struggling to hold it aloft any longer

"Gacking impressive," Torbon admired, grinning at the Ursite, who panted heavily and looked ready to fall over. Torbon stepped over and supported the big guy to keep that from happening.

The bladed droid twitched and spasmed where it fell, sparks sputtering out of dozens of gashes in its armored frame. Taj came over and stared down at the bot.

"These things are tough," she admitted, shaking her head. "It looks like it still wants to kill us."

"I'm sure it does," Dent confirmed, examining the fallen bot as it writhed on the ground, not yet ready to surrender.

"How are we gonna explain all this?" Lina asked, motioning toward the damaged droids, and then the wreckage outside the room in the hallway. There was blood visible everywhere out there, from the walls to the floor, and even the ceiling, where it dripped down like a crimson rain.

Cabe stuck his head out through the hole in the wall and whistled as he glanced both ways. Holding a hand over his mouth, he mumbled, "It's pretty ugly out here."

Taj stopped to listen and realized that she didn't hear alarms going off anywhere inside the palace. "We might have a few minutes to make something up," she said, calling their attention to the lack of alarm at the attack.

Once more her paranoia sparked up at the realization that nothing felt right about the attack and the lack of response on behalf of the Orgesse Clan.

Did someone there know the Furlorians weren't who they said they were, she wondered.

Then a muffled *beep* sounded.

The Furlorians stopped and glanced around, looking for the source. Dent found it, pointing to the damaged droid.

"The sound's coming from it," he stated, leaning into take a closer look as the *beep* sounded again. "Why is it—" he started, then bolted upright, stiffening suddenly. "Oh dear," he muttered.

Lina came over to stand alongside Dent and examined the droid quickly. She, too, straightened quickly and took a step away from the battle droid.

"We've got another problem," the engineer announced.

By that point, Taj had realized what had alarmed both the AI and her friend. "Rowl," she mumbled under her breath. "We need to get out of here. Now!"

"What's going on?" Torbon asked, his head tilted as he stared at the frantic group gathered around the droid.

"Self-destruct mechanism," Lina answered, moving away from the bot.

"Bomb!" Cabe clarified when Torbon didn't immediately react.

That sunk in clearly.

Torbon cursed and darted forward, snatching up Lina and carrying her toward the back bedroom where they'd disabled the alarms on the window. Taj waved the rest after them, and Dent closed off the rear as the group bolted to escape.

"Trigger your camo-programs," Taj shouted as she knocked the window open and went to climb out.

"No time for stealth!" Dent called, wrapping his arms around the whole crew and shoving them out the window.

Taj bit back a shriek at the unexpected push and found herself in midair, her crew scattered around her. Her tail jutted straight out as she fell.

Two things happened in rapid succession.

The first, the droid exploded in the room they'd just abandoned. Bursts of flame and debris sprayed from the window above, brightening the night as though it were day.

The second thing was that Taj realized her fall had slowed to the point that she settled on the ground as if she were a feather. The rest of the crew landed alongside her, clearly as surprised by the lack of impact as she was.

"What the gack?" Cabe asked, but Dent helped them to their feet as shards of glass and debris rained down over them.

"No time to explain the technical aspects of the anti-grav failsafe," the AI told them, ushering them forward. "Run!"

The crew did just that as the rooms they'd been assigned were rattled by a second explosion—Taj subconsciously thinking that was the first bot being set off—and the entire section of the palace was engulfed in fiery red and orange flames. Black smoke filled the air around the palace, crowding out the night sky.

Several more explosions sounded inside the palace, but Taj didn't have time to wonder what those might have been.

The guards on the wall ducked for cover and those on the ground scrambled to hide in the wake of the blasts. Taj and the crew clambered up the wall where there were no guards present, and Lina assured them that her earlier hack of the wall's security was still in place.

They landed on the other side, all eyes on the palace, and bolted to the same alleyway Taj had fled to the first time she'd snuck out of the palace. She wouldn't let them rest there, though, leading them up the wall and onto the roofs, having mapped out the safest spots out of sight from the street on her first journey.

None of them bothered to look back as the palace burned, but there was no doubt in Taj's mind that there would be consequences for what had happened there.

She initially thought about having the crew return to the palace, to speak with Queen Rilan and her people to explain themselves, but her paranoia nagged at her. First the ambush in the caravan, then the attack in the palace, neither of which the Orgesse Clan had seemed to put much effort into stopping.

It was clear the clan was involved or they'd been compromised somehow. Either way, the palace wasn't safe for the Furlorians. Someone was out to get them, but Taj gacking well wasn't going to let anything happen to her crew under her watch.

She'd accepted this mission to prove something to the Federation and show what her crew was capable of. And though she hadn't expected it to be so dangerous, and the General hadn't either, things had clearly changed. Unless he'd set them up and the test continued. But the death and destruction with the two ambushes made that less likely. She could not believe the Federation would throw away anyone's lives like they'd seen on this planet.

That took a level of malice that made her fur stand on end.

The crew was on the run from faceless enemies, and they needed to determine who the gack they were before things escalated even further. They needed someplace to hunker down and process everything, figure out a better plan of action to find and rescue Grom Hadar, and then go from there.

That in mind, Taj led them across the rooftops to Grom's hideout, hoping it hadn't been compromised since she'd left it.

But if it had been, she was okay with that.

Taj was in the mood to kick some more ass.

CHAPTER TEN

"The droids have failed," Vetrus announced, coming into the room where Skol Arduin sat, watching the image of the Orgesse Palace burning on the view screens.

"Of course they have," he said with a sigh, leaning back in his chair. He looked away from the screens and glanced at his right-hand man. "This is becoming a habit, it appears."

Vetrus nodded. "These Furlorians are more than they appear to be," he said, motioning back to the monitors. One of the screens flickered and a holo of the cats fighting against the battle droids appeared, the recording having been taken from the perspective of the bots.

"But *what* are they?" Skol questioned his man. "Have you gotten any answers from Grom?"

"No," Vetrus answered, not bothering to soften his answer for his boss. "He claims to know nothing of the Furlorians, nor is he claiming to have any evidence against Alshan Ra."

Skol grunted, a sneer peeling back his upper lip. "We know both to be untrue, but Alshan Ra doesn't want presumptions," he told his second, "he wants confirmation. Without it, he won't risk going after the Orgesse Clan openly. He can't afford to have Federation operatives interfere in his business."

"We're unlikely to get that confirmation from Grom Hadar no matter how hard we push him," Vetrus admitted. "The man is unexpectedly resistant to my probes. He's more likely to die first."

"Which means we need to focus on the Furlorians," Skol decided. "Does our agent have eyes on them?"

Vetrus shook his head. "They slipped free of the palace during the confusion. Our operative stymied the alarms before setting the bots loose, but there was no way to confirm anything from that end until after the attack had failed. By then, they'd vanished."

"Which means the Furlorians could be anywhere in Dulta by now." Skol growled and slammed a fist into the arm of his chair. "Alshan Ra is going to have our heads, Vetrus. We need to find these creatures before they stumble across any of our operations and connect the dots."

"We have the footage from the droids," Vetrus reminded Skol. "Can we use that to draw them out perhaps? Make it public?"

"And admit to Alshan Ra that we failed again?" Skol asked. "By all means, Vetrus. If you want to sacrifice yourself to take him bad news, go right ahead. Me..." Skol jabbed himself in the chest with his index finger. "I much prefer not dying."

"As do I," Vetrus agreed. "Still, we need to do something or Alshan Ra will eventually tire of our efforts and feel he needs to make an example of us."

Skol nodded. As much as he wanted to argue with Vetrus, he knew his right-hand man was correct. Alshan Ra had little patience for failure and, so far, that's all Skol had offered the man since they'd captured Grom Hadar, the double-agent who'd worked both sides of the Zoranthian war, and who threatened to expose Ra's greatest secret to the world.

With only the barest of intel gathered from Grom's possessions, pointing to possible interference by the Etheric Federation in Zoranthian politics, Skol had been tasked to learn more and to deal with the situation before it impacted Alshan Ra's plans.

So far, he'd done neither, and Skol was running out of time and opportunity, he knew.

"Reach out to our operative and make sure word is quietly spread that the Orgesse guests are more than they seem," Skol told Vetrus. "Sow the seeds of distrust in the wake of their disappearance so the Heltrol might be inclined to do more than simply find them. Then spread the word among our people and have them scour the city for these Furlorians, as well. Offer them whatever it takes to stir them to action."

"And when they find them?" Vetrus asked.

Skol chuckled. "If they can't be captured, then kill them," he answered.

"Don't we risk angering the Federation by doing so?"

"If they are Federation agents, then the Federation has decided not to operate openly here, even if it means they lose Grom. That makes me think they will not make a scene should something happen to either them or Grom. And if they're not agents, they're still in the way of the master's plans, by accident or intent."

Vetrus nodded along.

"Either way, they need to be dealt with before they cause us more problems." He waved his man off. "Find them, Vetrus. Find them."

Vetrus spun on his heel and left the room to follow his orders. Skol watched him leave, wondering just how he'd come to this point.

He'd been led to believe the visiting Furlorians were Etheric Federation agents because of Grom having reached out secretively to the Federation before Skol's men had captured him. The Furlorians had arrived immediately after that, and Skol felt it was too much of a coincidence.

Still, there was no proof of anything at this point.

Grom was a traitor, yes, and he was spotted by Alshan Ra at one of the convocations, but Skol had nothing beyond that to hold against the man. He needed to know more, needed more certainty, before he risked everything going after the Furlorians openly in an effort to appease his master.

Skol had to be sure he wasn't stirring a hornet's nest.

He rose from his seat and went to the elevator again.

It was time he questioned Grom Hadar himself.

CHAPTER ELEVEN

Grom's house was exactly as Taj had left it. She was a little conflicted by that but decided it was probably for the best that no one had stumbled across it since she'd last been there.

"This is...fancy," Torbon complained, spinning in a circle and taking in the tiny hovel of an apartment. He looked offended by all the dirt and dust.

"It's no palace, that's for sure," Cabe replied, plopping down on Grom's couch after sliding the pillow aside. The couch creaked beneath his weight.

"No room service, I'm guessing," Krawg said, dropping down beside Cabe.

"Sorry, big guy," Lina told him. "You'll have to fluff your own pillows and scavenge for food like the rest of us."

"Unfortunate," Krawg said, shaking his shaggy head.

"It's still better than being dead, right?" Taj asked.

The Ursite shrugged. "Marginally."

Taj grinned at Krawg's response. "Things could be worse."

"Tell that to my stomach," Torbon whined. "I knew we should have packed up the food and took it with us like Krawg suggested."

"Now it's spread over the palace walls, satisfying no one," Krawg joined in, obviously pouting. He slouched into the cushions.

"That's it, guys," Lina said, coming over to stand alongside Taj. "Way to stay positive."

"I can be positive," Torbon told her, waving his arms about. "I'm positive this place is a dump and we're likely to catch lice before we get out of here," he announced, giving her a thumbs up.

"I'm positive you're a gackwad," Lina countered, letting out a loud sigh.

"She's not wrong," Cabe chimed in. "You *are* a gackwad."

Torbon huffed. "And you're a…" he trailed off, thinking for a moment before giving up and going quiet.

Cabe laughed at Torbon, who growled back.

Taj glanced at Dent, eyebrow raised and whiskers flickering. "It's like babysitting a newborn litter," she told the AI before turning back to the crew. "Okay, that's enough, guys. We've got enough going on without being at each other's throats."

"I need to finish going over the scans," Dent announced, retreating to a corner of the room and sitting down cross-legged away from the rest of the crew so he wouldn't be distracted.

"The rest of us need to discuss our next move," Taj told them, coming over and plopping down on the floor in front of the crew. Lina joined her, and Torbon squeezed in alongside the Ursite, the two of them battling for space.

Taj motioned to the engineer first. "Are you still hooked into the system at the palace?"

A small monitor appeared on her forearm, and Lina nodded confirmation after a few minutes of data scrolling across the screen. "I'm still in, but they've adjusted their security protocols in the wake of the attack."

"What's that mean?" Taj asked.

"It's gonna take me a while to burrow past them to where I can get to more than the basic security operations I'd already messed with. My backdoor is still in place, since it was coded to be unobtrusive, but I'll need to do more setup work to access other aspects of the system."

Taj nodded. "Do it, please. We need to stay abreast of what's going on there," she said. "It's pretty clear they're gonna be suspicious when we aren't in our rooms and they don't find our bodies among the mess, and I'd like a heads up on what they're thinking or planning on doing, if possible."

"You expecting them to come looking for us?" Cabe asked.

"Definitely," she replied. "We're supposed to be pampered royals, remember? Our sudden vanishing act is gonna stir up a response of some sort."

She turned around and leaned against his legs, rubbing at her temples as she got comfortable.

"They'll either think we've been kidnapped and feel obligated to search for us to keep their hopes of Toradium-42 alive, or they'll think we're involved in an attack on the palace, which means they'll be looking for us with another ending in mind. Neither of which gives us much time to work without someone finding us eventually."

"We probably can't stay here very long either," Lina noted. "If Grom doesn't return soon, we have to believe he's not gonna, which likely means something bad has happened to him. Could mean this place is compromised. It's a risk to stay here."

Taj nodded her agreement. "You're right. We need to find someplace better to hide out, but we can't just abandon this place. Its connection to Grom means it might well be in play still, either by him or someone connected to him."

"We can plant a bug for after we leave," Cabe suggested.

"Gack!" Taj stiffened, sitting upright. "Speaking of bugs…"

"I scanned as soon as we entered, don't worry," Dent informed her.

Taj sank back with a relieved sigh. "I forgot to check the first time I was here. I could very well have led the bots back to the palace now that I'm thinking about it."

"Doubtful," Dent assured her. "Our unseen enemies already knew where we were. They didn't need to follow you to learn that, it's all over the news broadcasts in bold letters. Besides, the fact that you found these photos here makes it clear no one has invaded Grom's sanctuary besides us. That means there was no one to follow you."

Cabe set a hand on her shoulder, massaging the tension out of the muscles. "They knew we were coming from the start, so none of this is on you," he told her. "There's an informant somewhere, tattling on our every move, I'd bet."

"As would I," Lina agreed. "It makes sense that it's

someone connected to the palace as that was the only point of contact made by the Federation initially."

"Unless of course someone is spying on the Orgesse Palace," Dent countered, "which is also entirely likely. These people are at war with the entire world, remember. Their enemies are everywhere."

"Which leaves us guessing once more," Taj growled, not happy to still be in the dark regarding something so important.

"It's Rolkar," Torbon stated matter-of-factly. "I don't trust her."

Taj chuckled at his conviction. "I don't either, and she's as likely a suspect as anyone else, but we're just guessing at this point."

"She was in charge of our safety," Cabe argued. "Twice under her supposed protection, we were attacked and nearly killed. I'm thinking that excludes her from the soldier of the year award if nothing else."

"I agree, but—"

"I think I found something," Dent called out, getting up to join them, interrupting their discussion about Rolkar's guilt or innocence.

"You get a match on the man's face?" Taj asked.

"No," Dent answered, bringing up a screen on his forearm like Lina had done earlier, "I'm still running the data, but I'm drawing a blank on identification of the man in the images. However, I've managed to locate several nearby manufacturers who customize or build bots similar to those that attacked us." He shrugged. "That at least gives us someplace to examine while I continue to tap the local databases, which appear to be extremely slow and difficult thanks to the combative nature of the forces involved. Even their network systems are at war, it seems."

Taj sighed, wanting to complain but not. They still had a job to do. She clambered to her feet.

She'd imagined this mission being a simple seek, find, and rescue, her and the crew delivering Grom Hadar to the Federation without much in the way of drama. Of course, the mission had been nothing *but* drama from the start, and Taj was already tired of the hurdles being thrown their way.

She wanted the mission over.

"Let's take a look at these places, question the owners," Taj said.

"Checked the time lately?" Torbon asked her, tapping his wrist.

She hadn't even given the time a thought until he said something. She checked her eyepiece and groaned.

It was still hours before dawn.

"We could break in," Cabe suggested. "Search the place and see what we find."

"Probably not a good idea seeing how many people are probably out looking for us," Lina countered.

"But if we wait until morning, the Heltrol will have put two and two together if they have any sort of detective acumen and will be doing the same thing."

"That's a big *if*," Torbon argued.

"They can't be that incompetent if the Orgesse Clan is still in charge," she reminded him.

That thought, of course, only made her suspect Commander Rolkar's intentions even more, but even if the woman was a traitor, there was no way she would over-

look a clue as obvious as looking for battle droid manufacturers. Not if she didn't want to make it obvious she was
on the enemy's payroll.

"I think we need to risk it," Taj stated. "If we wait,
there's a chance that Rolkar, or whoever, has the time to
cover things up. Right now, so soon after the attack, there
might be evidence still sitting around."

Dent shrugged. "Without serial or part numbers from
the droids, which I'm sure were wiped clean from their
systems and frames, it's a shot in the dark that we'll find
anything incriminating."

"Now who's being negative?" Torbon teased.

"Simply stating facts," Dent answered.

"Well, regardless, I can't just sit here and do nothing,"
Taj said. "I'm going."

"Déjà vu," Krawg muttered. "I'm going as well. Anything
has to be better than sitting around in this hovel."

"I think it's best we all go, if any of us are," Dent told
the crew.

Taj grinned, grateful to have her whole crew this time.
She turned to Lina. "Work up a bug with audio and video
and plant it somewhere good," she said. "I want to know if
anyone comes in after us."

Lina started in immediately, and Taj decided on their
plan of action.

It wasn't much of a plan, she had to admit, but it was all
they had.

And then it really wasn't.

The nearest of the bot manufacturers had been a bust from the start. It might as well have been a junkyard for all the usable parts it had on hand. Everything was rusted and rundown and battered so badly that there was no way to even call the equipment secondhand. It was fifth or sixth, at best.

But the place was huge.

The shop was established in a giant warehouse with a massive field of clutter out back, and it took the crew hours to weave their way through the whole place after Lina had cracked the miniscule security the place had.

It was more like a hoarder's paradise than anything resembling an operational droid shop.

Lina and Dent had hacked the owner's servers and searched for anything that might point to the place being involved in the droid attack, but there was simply nothing there outside of a number of shady deals where the owner had gone out of his way to skimp on paying his taxes.

While the Orgesse Clan might well find that egregious, Taj didn't give a gack.

The second location was far more difficult to access than the first.

More centralized in Dulta, the shop was modern and well-maintained. The sun was just coming up as the crew arrived. Traffic had yet to start moving in the streets around the shop, but Taj knew they were running out of time to search the place.

Dent had determined the shop wouldn't open for another four hours or so, meaning no one was likely to show up right away, but breaking in during daylight hours wasn't exactly the brightest of maneuvers.

Taj, of course, did it anyway.

Lina and Dent struggled to get past the security systems, which gave Taj hope that they'd found the right spot. After the slum of the last place, it seemed entirely reasonable that the second shop had beefed up security because it had something to hide.

It did, but it wasn't what Taj had been looking for.

The shop was largely a cover for the owner's drug operation.

Taj sighed as she stumbled across a hidden cache of illegal narcotics stuffed inside the frames of droids, which were being shipped off-world.

At first, Taj had gotten excited. Surely a drug dealer would be interested in making battle droids for someone interested in a kidnapping or assassination attempt, but Dent disappointed her with what he'd found.

While the owner was definitely a criminal, the shop wasn't designed to do more than build the basic frame-work of the bots. It had none of the complicated elec-tronics on hand to create the intelligence systems or the coding above a basic level.

"This isn't the place," the AI told her with no uncertainty.

So, they snuck out and avoided the growing traffic around the building and trekked off to the last of the shops on Dent's list. By then, the work day was in full swing in the city of Dulta.

Several times, Taj and the crew had to hide from Heltrol soldiers as they patrolled the streets. The soldiers stopped and interviewed people at random, and Taj caught a snippet of conversation regarding the crew.

She gnashed her teeth and swore under her breath.

"That answers that," Torbon said over the comm.

Dent agreed, tapping the side of his head. "Chatter tells me that the Orgesse Clan is paying a handsome reward for any information regarding us," he informed them. "It appears we are being implicated in the attack upon the Heltrol stationed outside of our room as well as an attack elsewhere in the palace."

"Seriously?" Taj snarled, suddenly glad she hadn't returned to the palace like she'd first been inclined to. "If it wasn't clear there's someone on the inside stirring things up, it most certainly is now."

"Unless one of you snuck off and killed someone in the palace when the rest of us weren't looking," Torbon challenged jokingly, raising an eyebrow and looking at each crewmember in turn as if to catch some hint of guilt.

"If we were gonna kill anyone, Torbon, it would have been you," Cabe told him.

"We're obviously being set up," Lina stated.

"Gacking Rolkar," Torbon muttered.

"Speaking of whom," Dent called out, drawing their attention across the street to where the last of the three shops on his list sat.

There, in front of the shop, was a Heltrol squad, armed and armored and clearly ready for anything. At its head was Commander Rolkar.

"At least she's pretending to do her duty," Lina sniped, biting back a low growl.

"Of course she has to do it right now," Cabe complained. "Do you think she'll find anything while she's here?"

Taj shrugged. "I'm not even sure she's looking for anything but us," she told him.

Camo-program active on their suits, the crew sat back away from the edge to be safe, then waited. Just a few minutes later, Commander Rolkar and her crew exited the shop and marched off in a huff.

"We spent more time in the junkyard than they did here," Torbon stated, shaking his head. "The commander just looks guiltier and guiltier."

Taj couldn't help but agree. No matter how cooperative the shop owner might have been, there was no way the Heltrol could have examined the droids on hand and come to a true conclusion that they weren't involved.

That meant either she was covering for the owner or for herself.

Either possible, Taj decided they need to talk to the shop owner themselves and see what he had to say.

She turned to face Dent. "Can the suit imitate the Heltrol outfit?" she asked.

"I don't see why not," he answered. "It obviously can't adjust your real face to give you four eyes."

"But if I process a helmet, it can mimic the complete look, right?"

Dent thought for a second and nodded. "I believe so, though it might not stand up to close examination."

Taj grinned. "Good enough for me."

"Wait!" Cabe called out. "What are you gonna do?"

"I'm gonna go talk to the guy."

In the blink of an eye, her suit changed shape, taking on the form of a Heltrol soldier. She mimicked the commander rank on her arms to add some authority, grinning as the crew stared at her, wide-eyed.

"That's kinda creepy," Lina told her. "The suit accessorized the eyes behind the visor perfectly."

"It's like you're staring into my soul," Krawg muttered, backing away and raising his hands in surrender. "I don't like it."

"So, I'll pass for Heltrol?" Taj asked with a chuckle.

"Without a doubt," Cabe said, nodding at her. "It really is creepy. I hope you get stuck looking like this."

Taj grinned and leaned toward him. "C'mon, baby, give me a kiss."

Cabe covered his mouth with his hand. "Pass, thanks."

Taj laughed and glanced over the edge of the building. "Anyone going with me?" She turned around to see Dent having altered his suit to imitate hers.

"I think it best that just you and I go," he suggested. "Too many of us attempting to mimic the Heltrol outfits and I believe someone will notice a discrepancy, especially since there is no way to alter the appearance of height." He glanced at Krawg as he said it.

"I'm perfectly fine with that," the Ursite answered.

Taj agreed. "Let's go then before any real Heltrol find a reason to come back."

She slipped over the side of the wall where no one could see her and triggered the anti-grav fall system Dent had used earlier when they'd fled the castle. She grinned as she alighted gently on the floor.

You'll have to show me the rest of the tricks, Dent, she told the AI over the mental link.

When we have sufficient time to train you in them, I most certainly will.

The pair strode across the street, and Taj was glad to see people going out of their way to avoid them. The locals didn't want much to do with the royal guard, it seemed, and that was fine by Taj.

Dent opened the shop door for Taj, befitting her higher rank, and the two marched inside. The shop was small compared to the previous one, kind of a mix between the first and the second, but it was clear its technology level was sufficient to create droids like the ones that had attacked the crew.

An open alcove led to the main part of the shop past a counter covered in holo-mags of bot designs. Work was going on across several assembly lines, and Taj could see much of the process of droid assembly at work.

These were full bots, too, heads and operating systems being installed while she watched.

"Again?" a man complained, slipping off the work floor and coming to stand behind the counter. "Didn't I already answer all your damn questions?" he asked.

Dressed in simple coveralls, the man glared at Dent and Taj with all four of his yellow eyes. His lip was peeled back in a sneer, his dark hair slicked back across his scalp. He looked angry and somewhat threatening, broader across the chest and arms than most of the Zoranthians Taj had seen since landing on the planet.

She gasped as she stared, but it was the man's presence she was reacting to.

"Actually," she answered, managing to not stutter.

"You're right, you have." She spun on her heel and marched toward the door without another word.

"He has?" Dent asked, glancing back and forth between the two, clearly confused by Taj's declaration.

The shop owner only looked slightly less confused than Dent did, clearly not having expected his brusque attitude to have worked so well at chasing the would-be guards away.

"Thank you for your time, citizen," Taj called out and stormed from the shop, Dent on her heels. She didn't wait for him as she crossed the street and slipped into the alley.

"What is it?" Dent asked, catching up to her. "You didn't even ask him anything," he argued.

Taj turned and faced him, grinning. "I didn't have to."

Dent waited a moment for more, then finally nudged Taj when she didn't say anything. "And?"

"That, my friend, is called acting," she told him with a wink. "A dramatic pause for impact."

"Uh…" Dent blinked.

"Anyway," Taj went on, clearly seeing the AI's confusion, "I didn't need to ask the owner anything." She triggered the holo her eyepiece had captured of the room and sent it over to Dent.

The AI watched the short holo-clip, eyes going wide as it played. "The symbols behind him on the wall…" he said quietly.

"Exactly," Taj confirmed. "Just like those in Grom's photos."

She grinned.

"We've got him."

CHAPTER TWELVE

The crew settled in and spent the rest of the day watching the shop.

Lina had set up tiny cameras to keep eyes on the sides and back of the building in case the owner tried to sneak out, and then they waited. And waited, and waited.

As morning turned into late afternoon, Dent went out in disguise to find the crew something to eat, as Krawg and Torbon whined incessantly until they were fed. Dent was happy to get something, if only to shut the pair up.

After that, night came on slowly. Camped out on the roof with their camo-programs running so no one nearby could see them without being right on top of the group, they'd gotten comfortable in their stakeout. Several of the crew had fallen asleep even, but Taj and Lina kept Dent company as the hours wore on.

"Does this guy live here?" Lina complained, finally losing her patience. "All his employees have left, all the systems have been shut down, and this guy is hanging around hours after all that."

"Maybe he knows we're here," Taj answered, offering the engineer a tired shrug.

"Doubtful," Dent argued. "It's more likely that he's waiting on someone or something. The Heltrol put so little effort into questioning him that I can't picture the man being spooked."

"Maybe we did, though," Taj said.

"Also doubtful," he replied. "Coming so soon on the heels of the first Heltrol officers, he likely believed we were simple foot soldiers who hadn't realized he'd already been questioned. Reviewing the holo of his actions, he never once glanced at your rank or mine."

"Which is a good thing, as we would have looked like even bigger idiots to him," Taj grunted.

"That's a good thing, though," Lina clarified. "Either Rolkar is protecting him or she and her people are incompetent, as we've discussed. Both are likely to set him at ease."

"Then why the gack is he still in there?" Taj complained. "We've been here all day and learned absolutely nothing." She gestured to Lina's wrist and opened her mouth to say something else, but the engineer cut her off.

"The answer is still no," she said. "No one has gone into Grom's place since we've been here."

Taj sighed.

The streets dark below, Taj scanned the area for the millionth time, watching the few wandering homeless tread down the street again, which they'd done since the sun started to set.

Once more, she couldn't imagine living like that, nowhere to go to feel safe or sheltered. It hurt her heart to picture anyone she knew living that way, and she wondered if there was something she could do to help them.

She was contemplating what that might be when she spied movement across the street at the droid shop. Lights flickered inside, and the door swung open.

"About gacking time," Lina growled.

Taj leaned forward and peered over the edge of the building, watching as the owner stepped outside and closed the door behind him. He carried a small duffel bag in one hand, and he triggered the building's security with a swipe of his palm on a panel beside the door. Then he started off down the street after taking a quick glance at his surroundings and apparently finding nothing to alarm him.

Lina woke the rest of the crew as Taj stood and stretched, every joint and muscle aching from the long period of being cramped up and hunched down.

"You got him?" she asked Dent, and the AI nodded. He leapt across the roof without waiting for anyone else. "I'm going to follow him. Join me once the crew is roused and ready."

Taj watched him go, nodding at his back as if he could see her. She turned around once Dent disappeared and waved the crew on.

"Let's go, people," she ordered. "Wakey, wakey."

"I don't wanna," Torbon whined, stumbling to his feet and wavering as he stretched, yawning widely.

"We finish the mission, then you can go home and sleep

in a comfortable bed, eat all the food you want, and not have to worry about battle droids breaking in and trying to kill you," Taj told him.

"That was almost motivational," Cabe told her, chuckling under his breath.

"Practice makes perfect," she said, once more motioning for them to get moving. "Let's go. Don't want Dent getting too far away."

"Can't have that now, can we?" Torbon muttered, walking over to the ledge of the building and glancing down at the street below. "Can we rent a hover-cab?"

Taj grunted. "I wish." Then she leapt across the intervening space between the buildings, landing on the neighboring roof.

She didn't need to look back to see if the rest of the crew had followed her, her scanners assured her that they had. So, she continued on, chasing Dent's signal. The AI had been moving relatively slowly as he stalked the shop owner, whose name they had determined to be Jal Doro after searching the city's servers.

Jal took his time wherever he was going, and Taj and the others caught up to Dent before long, while Jal continued casually on his way.

Any idea where he's going? Taj asked, resorting to the mental link out of paranoia more than any real chance that the shop owner could hear her on the roof.

"Only that he's leading us in the general direction of Grom Hadar's hideout," he answered using the comm.

Taj watched as the man walked below, moving as though he were out for an evening stroll. Considering the neighborhood he was traveling through, Taj had to admire his confidence. It was clear he either belonged there or he knew something the resident bad influences didn't, which made him feel comfortable walking through such an area with no obvious way to defend himself.

Finally, after following Jal to the edge of town, he slowed at a corner and glanced around furtively, showing the first sign of nervousness since he'd left his shop. A moment later, once he was apparently satisfied he was alone, which made Taj chuckle, he slipped around the corner and marched straight toward a recessed door in the building across the way. The crew followed above.

At the door, Jal knocked with a hesitant, rhythmic motion. He leaned against the wall while he waited, doing his best to appear casual, but he didn't pull it off well. And seeing that only made Taj think she'd made the right decision to follow him. He finally looked as if he were doing something he shouldn't be, and that had to be a good thing for Taj and her crew.

A few long moments later, the door eased open without a sound, and Taj spied a man in black robes hovering behind the door, doing his best to remain out of sight. He waved Jal in without saying a word and shut the door immediately afterward.

"See the robes?" Taj asked.

Dent nodded. "I did indeed."

"This is the place then?" Cabe asked.

"Looks that way," she answered, staring down at the sealed door Jal had gone through. "The only question now is how we go about getting inside."

The best thing about secretive societies," Lina

explained, grinning all the while, "is that they are secretive."

"Insightful," Krawg muttered.

"My point being," Lina went on, "is that they don't operate in places where there is a lot of traffic." She waved her arm about, gesturing toward the silent, dark street below. "No one's gonna notice if we go down there and knock on the door like good ol' Jal did."

Dent nodded his agreement. "I'm not picking up any security systems on the building or door, and I don't even see a peephole on it. No one inside will know who is knocking if we use their code."

"Except if everyone who's showing up is already there," Taj argued, but she was certain it was still the best idea. "Let's do it."

Taj pointed to Lina. "Stick around up here and watch the door and let us know if anyone is coming, okay?"

Lina snarled but agreed without arguing.

Taj gave the engineer a quick hug, whispering in her ear, "You're the only one I trust to watch our backs."

Lina snorted at the obviously false reassurance, not bothering to reply, and the crew slipped over the side of the building and made their way across the street. They slipped over in front of the door and stepped to the side of it as Taj imitated Jal's rhythmic knock.

She waited impatiently as time crept by, wondering if a plan so simple as knocking on a door was going to back-fire. A minute later, however, she heard the bolts being drawn inside, and the door swung open just as it had for Jal, no questions asked.

A pale man in black robes stared out at her with four

eyes, all of which narrowed with recognition an instant later. He opened his mouth to shout, but Taj struck him neatly in the jaw. His four eyes rolled back, and he collapsed. Dent caught him before he hit the ground, slipping inside with the fallen man and setting him against the wall.

"Nice punch," Cabe complimented.

"Helps having powered armor," she said, but she couldn't keep from grinning. It felt good to punch the man.

The rest of the crew stepped inside and shut the door behind them, locking it. A long corridor stretched out from the door, and Taj could hear muted voices in the distance. Like the secret knock, there was a rhythm to it that seemed almost musical, as if the voices were chanting.

Taj started off toward the sound.

"We just leaving him here?" Cabe asked.

"He'll be out for a while," Dent assured, grabbing the man's chin and turning his head to both sides while scanning him. "He has a solid concussion and won't be much of a worry as long as we're not here overly long."

Cabe shrugged and followed after Taj. Torbon tailed along without arguing, and Dent brought up the rear.

All clear out here, Lina reported. *Seems no one even noticed you.*

That's a good thing, Taj answered back. *All good in here, too.*

Lina cut communications at that and let the crew get on with their task.

Taj crept through the hallway, careful where she placed every footstep to avoid making a sound. The rest of the crew followed her lead until Dent chuckled in their ears over the comm.

"You do realize that the suits employ sound-suppressing technology, yes?" he asked from behind them, watching their every move with amusement. "Unless you go out of your way to make a bunch of noise, stomping your feet, striking the walls, no one is going to hear you coming," he explained.

"Now you tell us," Torbon grunted, straightening and stretching.

"We need a full training on these suits and their capabilities," Taj mumbled, remembering when she'd clung to the wall while sneaking out of the palace. She'd been so afraid the guard would hear her then, only she hadn't needed to be worried about it at all, even though the guards had said they heard something. She wondered how it worked so she could be certain.

"You need only ask," Dent replied with a shrug.

"That's convenient," Taj groaned, waving the crew on. They didn't have time to get into a discussion about what the suits could and couldn't do right then, and she sure didn't want to give Torbon the opportunity to start quizzing Dent. They'd be there all day if that happened.

Taj slipped to the edge of the hallway and peeked furtively around the corner. She nearly gasped at what she saw.

Almost exactly like Grom Hadar's pictures, a cluster of men gathered in the center of the room just the other side of where Taj crouched. They wore the same black robes the man at the door had, as well as those seen in the photos.

Their voices rose in an awkward, but surprisingly melodic, wave, the words coming out as gibberish, Taj's translator not understanding any of them.

She glanced about, spying more of the symbols she had seen in the photos and at Jal's shop. She looked to find the droid shop owner, but there was no way to tell him apart from the others.

The man in the center was the only one who stood out as different.

Taj zeroed in on his exposed face as he stood in silent reflection, recognizing him as the same man she'd seen before. He carried the same book, and though she could see it better this time around, there was nothing on its cover she could use to identify it.

She let her suit record the scene playing out before her, making sure to zoom in on the man's lowered features, as well as all the symbols she could see in order to have a decent recording, should she need them. She also made sure the sound was recording, so she could translate what they were saying at some point.

What the gack are they doing? Torbon asked, inching over by Taj so he could see directly and not just catch a feed of what Taj was witnessing and passing back to them. *This is some ritualistic shaman-type gack, looks like.*

Taj had to agree. *I don't know what they're doing,* she admitted, shaking her head. *It looks...strange.*

Dent moved behind them and watched over their shoulders. Taj heard him mutter a, *Hmmm. I think we're about to find out what they're doing,* he said.

Just after he said that, the man in the middle lifted his chin and called out something indecipherable, raising his hands, clasping his book in one. The chanting stopped at that, and the room went silent. A chill tickled Taj's spine at his easy command of all those gathered about him.

They looked up at him rapturously. She could see it even through the masks that hid their faces and expressions from her. Their body language was enough for her to know what they felt. They swayed on their knees like serpents under the spell of a flute.

The man stood before them and smiled, taking in his supplicants.

"Our time is at hand," he said in clear Zoranthian, the crew's translators adjusting so they could understand everything he said now that it recognized the language. "The Queen Worm still sits upon her throne, believing herself immune to the voices of the people who would cast her down."

Does he mean Queen Rilan? Torbon asked over the link. *Is that why they attacked us in the caravan?*

Taj shrugged, waving him to silence so she could listen.

"Long has she ruled over those greater than herself and dragged the people of Dulta into ruin behind her." The man rose up even taller and lifted a hand before his disciples, fingers hooked like talons. "We must take what is ours, brothers. Bring down the crown and stand above, proud in the ashes of her failure."

He paced in front of the men on their knees, poking a finger at each one in turn as he passed. "We are the martyrs called upon by the great Elerus to bring blood to the people, to rain war down on the oppressors. We are the blade, destined to strike deep into the heart of the Worm!

"Sharpen thy hands, my brothers! Prepare thy souls to meet our goddess Elerus. Make ready to—"

We've got a problem, guys, Lina said over the comm, speaking loudly over the fiery sermon, drowning it out.

Taj bit back a hiss at the poorly-timed interruption. *What is it?*

Incoming, Taj fired back. *Four men at the door. They have a key. They're coming inside. I can't take them out without making a huge scene out here.*

"Rowl," Taj muttered under her breath. She glanced around, looking for another way out.

There was none.

Backward or forward? Cabe asked, realizing the situation they were in.

They're in, Lina confirmed.

And here we forgot to clean up after ourselves, Krawg said, letting out a whispery sigh.

There was a shout down the corridor behind them just after the Ursite spoke, and Taj glanced up to see the man in the middle of the gathering staring at her just as he did Grom in the last photo.

Her heart thumped at the clear malevolence exuded by his four eyes.

"Back!" Taj ordered, willing her weapon out of her suit and snapping off a couple of shots into the room in hopes of forcing everyone under cover.

She realized her mistake a split-second after she pulled the trigger.

Several of the robed men leapt to their feet and tackled their master, driving him to the ground beneath the shelter of their bodies, making it impossible to see him, let alone target him.

The rest, nearly fifteen by Taj's quick count, spun around and charged toward the crew without any hesitation. They screamed and howled, and Taj caught the glint of steel as knives were whipped free of hidden sheaths.

Dent was the first one down the hall, headed toward the door they'd come in through.

They're armed, Taj warned. *Be careful.*

Too late, Dent answered, and Taj saw what he meant.

The first of the new arrivals stepped forward with an almost suicidal glee warping his expression. He drove a foot-long blade into Dent's side, sliding it between the ribs until the hilt struck manufactured bone. Blood and ooze bubbled out of the wound over the man's hand.

Taj gasped as she watched, only remembering Dent was an AI in an android body when he grabbed the man's wrist and snapped it, ripping the blade out of his side without a sound as he did so.

The man, however, shrieked until Dent headbutted him into unconsciousness.

Dent shoved the man toward his companions and charged ahead to face the next one.

Torbon ducked past Dent and triggered his energy blades.

"Mine are bigger than yours," he shouted, slashing at the attacker before him.

Two crimson lines welled at his chest, and he stumbled into the man behind him while Torbon and Dent pushed on.

Cabe slithered around Taj, putting him between her and the men racing maniacally toward them.

"Stop being a hero, gack it!" she shouted, firing a blast over her shoulder to slow the men's advance.

"There needs to be something good carved on my head-stone," he answered, letting loose a barrage of gunfire that dropped the first of the men and slowed the rest as they scrambled to get past his body. "I sure wish I had my bolt rifle," he complained as he pushed into Taj and nudged her forward.

She did, too, but it had been too unwieldy for the suit to absorb properly. They were all stuck with pistols and wrist blades, and while both were better than nothing, it would have been nice to have better firepower.

Torbon hacked another of the men up front, and Dent blasted the last of them. The AI grabbed the nearest of them and threw him aside, clearing the way for the rest of the crew.

Taj and Cabe jumped over the prone body of the man she'd knocked out when they'd come in—him still oblivious to what was going on—and the pair bolted out the door behind the AI and Torbon, Krawg making sure they were protected from the rear.

Lina ran up to them as soon as they were clear and filled the doorway with bursts of fire before joining the crew as they bolted down the street.

"Any idea where we're going?" Lina asked as she came up alongside Taj.

"That way," Taj said, pointing straight ahead.

"Works for me," Lina answered.

And they ran.

CHAPTER THIRTEEN

"Which way?" Torbon asked after they'd run a long way, the men still chasing them like rabid hounds with the scent of blood in their noses.

"Here," Taj answered, huffing into the comm.

She darted to the left and bolted down a narrow alley. They'd managed to keep ahead of their pursuers, but the men were relentless. Taj hadn't wanted to engage with them beyond what was necessary, but she was starting to think they weren't going to have a choice soon. The men kept coming.

They'd run a long distance through the town already, Taj leading the way through as many back alleys and dark, deserted streets as she could. There'd been a few witnesses to the chase, but they had fled in the opposite direction, unwilling to become involved.

Taj couldn't blame them.

She didn't want to be involved.

Just as she was readying to tell the crew to find a defensive position from where they could take the men out, she spotted a crowd of people milling around a building a short distance to their left. The sounds of merriment and loud voices rose into the night.

"This way," she called out, veering down a narrow street toward the rambunctious crowd.

"Is this a good idea?" Lina asked, seeing the oblivious throng ahead. "People could get hurt because of us."

"We just need a distraction," she answered, ducking into a nearly-obscured alley off the main road. "Cover your faces so no one recognizes us," she ordered.

The rest did as she asked and followed her but almost missed her next turn into a narrow alcove that led into a nearby building. A man at the door shouted something incomprehensible at them as they stormed past his post, but that was the extent of his effort. His voice faded behind them as they wound their way through the labyrinth of hallways that splayed out before them.

Taj could hear the crowd roaring, the sound echoing through the stones of the building as they kept on, finally slowing as the hallways began to fill with people and become crowded. They pushed through a short distance longer before breaking into a massive, domed-ceiling room where hundreds of people gathered in small groups around the walls and at every corner.

"Where are we?" Torbon asked.

Taj shrugged. She had no idea, but she knew it was their best bet to lose the zealots—which was really the only reasonable name to give them—before the crew was forced into a firefight in the streets.

That wouldn't do good things for their effort not to be noticed by the authorities or anyone else.

Not able to see the knife-wielding zealots anywhere behind them, Taj went over to a barred alcove and stood before the open gate to catch her breath. The rest of the crew joined her, everyone but Dent panting heavily. The sound of the crowd was nearly deafening where they hunkered down.

I think we lost them, Cabe said over the link so he could be heard over the noise, staring back the way they'd come.

"About gacking time," Torbon shouted. "I'm tired of running."

"These suits do wonders for your strength and power, but they don't do a ton for cardio," Lina complained, leaning against Torbon.

"I'll see what I can do in revision," Dent told her, keeping watch as the crew reclaimed their wind.

"You do that," she shot back, giving him a thumbs-up.

"Rowl but this place is loud," Taj mumbled, mostly to herself as she straightened to take a better look around.

That was when the gate behind them creaked open and several gnarled, bent men pulled them through before they'd even realized what was going on.

"You're up next," one of the men told them, his breath like sewage on a hot summer's day.

Taj was glad for her mask right then as she struggled to make sense of what the man meant.

Another of the men slammed the gate closed, and Taj heard the bolt catch, locking them on this side as her mind started reeling.

"Wait!" she called out, pushing the foul man aside so she could think. "What is this?"

"The queue," the man answered, gesturing down the short, wide corridor that ended in an archway.

Bright light filled the arch, forcing her suit to adapt to its unexpected brilliance after having wandered the gloomy catacombs of the building.

"You're next, like I said," the man repeated while he and his compatriots pressed forward, forcing the crew along with them.

They reached the archway and Taj blinked as she saw a field of sand spread out before them.

"Next for what?" she asked.

"To fight, of course."

As he said that, the man and his helpers shoved the crew through the archway. A great metal portcullis slammed shut as soon as they were out, kicking up sand and blocking their path back the way they'd come.

The crew turned and stared at the gnarled men grinning behind the bars of the portcullis.

"Did he say fight?" Torbon asked, his tail twitching and slapping his leg.

"I'm fairly certain he did," Dent confirmed.

The man who'd been talking all along jabbed a nubby finger their way and pointed behind them.

"Might want to face that away 'fore you spend your round getting shot in the back."

As his words sunk in, the crew turned slowly and looked out at the vast expanse of space before them that they had been too distracted to notice right away.

"Oh...gacking Rowl!" Lina muttered, eyes so wide they reflected the array of bright lights beaming down on them.

"This is...unfortunate," Krawg said, staring out at the crowd that stared back at them, roaring.

"This is the..." Cabe started.

"The arena," Taj finished, her eyes taking in the spectacle before her. "We. Are. So. Gacked," she muttered as she realized how many citizens of Dulta were likely in the arena, and all eyes were on them.

"Well, if it's any consolation," Dent told them, "at least our faces are obscured."

"Are the fights televised?" Taj asked.

"I don't believe so," Dent answered, "which is another point in our favor. The men following us will need to be in the arena to know we are here, and I suspect men wielding knives won't be allowed into the crowd unless they are..." Dent trailed off.

"In the fighting area with us," Taj finished for him, shaking her head.

She glanced behind them but didn't see the zealots' faces peeking past the bars, just the amused eyes of the old men.

The crowd started to boo at the crew's hesitation.

"Best get on out there, folks," the gnarled old man told them. "You'll want the crowd on your side seeing how it's them that decides if you live or die when you lose. Don't wanna be pissing them off none."

"No, of course we don't," Taj conceded with a sneer.

"Why'd we take on this mission again?" Cabe asked.

"Because we're stupid," Torbon replied.

"I don't remember being asked," Krawg argued. "I'm

thinking I'll need to see some hazard pay if I'm going to be fighting in an arena."

The crew inched out onto the sand and into the dominion of the lights. Taj sucked in a deep breath when she realized just how big the arena was. There had to be ten thousand people or more there, each and every one of them staring down on the crew and expecting violence.

But what are we expected to fight? she asked herself, and the great clanking of another portcullis rising across the arena gave her an answer.

It wasn't the one she wanted.

"So much for my wish of it being a two-legged balboran with a limp," Torbon whined as their opponent made its way onto the sands.

Taj swallowed hard as she watched their opponent march into the arena to a cavalcade of applause. As it came to stand at the edge of the sand, its long shadow stretched to where they stood.

"Oh…dear," Dent mumbled, taking the thing in. "It's an automaton."

"Yeah, because I really wanted to know what the giant thing that's gonna crush us is called," Torbon whimpered, craning his neck to stare up at the massive mechanical beast.

. The automaton looked like a giant statue made of bronze, the arena's lights gleaming off its metal skin. Over ten meters tall—10.0584 to be exact, Taj's eyepiece informed her—it towered over the sands, the crew looking like tiny ants in comparison.

The crowd cheered, "Warpath! Warpath! Warpath!"

Their voices echoed through the arena, the sandy floor trembling in time to the chant.

"And it has a name," Cabe sighed. "Yay."

"And everyone knows it," Lina added, "which means it wins a lot. Nobody remembers the losers."

"I'm motivated now," Cabe grunted, unable to look away from the automaton.

"At least we're not fighting it alone," Dent said, pointing along the circle of the arena where handfuls of other warriors gathered, staring up at the giant mechanoid. "That's something."

Taj looked over at the other groups of warriors making ready to fight the automaton and groaned. They looked no more enthused than her crew did, and they looked far less capable.

"We are *so* dead."

"Hey!" Torbon complained. "That's my line."

"Warriors!" a great voice cried out, amplified throughout the arena.

It drew their attention to a small man who stood upon a floating platform high above the sandy floor. Massive view screens loomed behind him, magnifying his image so everyone in the crowd could see him as easily as they could hear him.

Dressed in colorful garb and wearing what appeared to be a top hat with the Orgesse Clan symbol sewed onto it, the man had a long, scraggly beard that seemed to swallow his mouth when he closed it.

His bright yellow eyes stared out over the sands.

"Steel your nerves for you face the automaton Warpath!"

The crowd drowned the man out for a few moments as they howled and cheered and clapped and made all sorts of noise that made Taj feel a little bit badly.

"These people sure do want to see us die," Taj remarked.

"Seems to be a trend since we arrived," Lina commented. "Maybe this mission was a bad idea."

"I told you so," Krawg said.

Taj spun on him. "No, you didn't!"

"Well, I would have had I known what was going to happen," he clarified, shrugging. "Pretty much the same thing."

"It's not remotely the same thing," Cabe argued.

"I'm with furry," Torbon stated.

Taj sighed as the bearded man on the floating platform went on.

"Today, we will see who the great Elerus favors."

"There's that name again," Dent said.

"It appears even the gods want us dead," Torbon whined.

"We're in good company then, seeing how Elerus apparently wants the queen dead, too," Lina said. "We just happen to be first, it appears."

"It's good to be the queen," Cabe announced.

"Not if the zealots and their master have their way," Taj corrected.

"True," Cabe replied with a shrug.

"Now is your time!" the bearded man screamed. "Let us see who the gods favor this day!"

A reverberating claxon rang out, stirring the crowd into a frenzy, and the automaton lifted one massive foot and took a step forward. Not unexpectedly, none of the warriors rushed out to meet it.

Taj groaned. While she didn't really want to see anyone lose their life, she had to admit she was a little disappointed when no one rushed off and took down the metal beast before she had to take it on.

"Where's a hero when you need one?" she asked no one in particular.

"Sadly," Dent answered, "I don't believe there are any in residence today."

He gestured to the other warriors still gathered about the portcullises they'd come in through. Most stood still, likely in shock, and stared up at the slowly approaching monstrosity as if they planned to just wait for it to arrive and crush them into pulp.

One man climbed onto the bars and screamed to be let out, beating his fist and forehead against the steel with a fervor.

"That one is most definitely not him," Dent went on, pointing to the man as he knocked himself unconscious and toppled to the sand at the base of the portcullis.

"Lucky him," Taj said, taking a step out into the arena. Applause rose at her back as the crowd noticed her. "I guess it's up to us."

She really, really wished it wasn't.

"You do realize we can flee at any time, right?" Dent said, tapping himself on his chest.

"Wait! What?" Torbon mumbled coming over to stand in front of Dent accusingly. "Why didn't you say that earlier?"

"I kind of assumed you wanted to stay or you would

have left already." Dent shrugged. "You could jump and climb out whenever you like."

"Now you tell me," Torbon growled. "I nearly soiled myself," he admitted.

"Fortunately, the suit would filter it and keep you dry so no one would be the wiser if you actually did."

"That's good to know," Cabe said and looked down at his crotch. "Handy."

"We're staying," Taj said, drawing all eyes to her.

"Uh, and why would we want to do that?" Torbon challenged. "You can see that giant robot-thing over there, right?" He pointed a shaky finger at the automaton.

Taj nodded. "I also see them and them and them," she answered, pointing at the small groups of warriors in the arena alongside them.

"Not our fault they don't have an awesome AI buddy who can whip them up cool toys to keep themselves alive," Torbon countered, patting Dent on the shoulder as if looking for backup with his argument.

"No, but we can't leave them here to die like this," Taj told him.

"Sure we can," Torbon argued, but Taj could see his will breaking down. He was simply arguing to argue at this point, mostly because he was scared.

And so was she, but she wouldn't let that stop her protecting those who needed it the most. There was no way she could look herself in the eye if she ran away and let these people be killed by the cruel, unfeeling creature that continued its advance toward the center of the arena.

"I forgot my cape," Torbon tried again, his eyes narrow and desperate.

"No, you didn't," Dent told him, and a long cape appeared out of the back of Torbon's suit. It fluttered in the soft breeze. "It's right there."

"I'm not liking you much right now, Dent" Torbon told the AI.

"We need to decide what we're doing soon," Cabe announced, gesturing to the automaton. "Big boy there is closing in fast."

"Then we take it down." Taj marched forward, head held high to mask the thrumming of her chest as her heart spasmed to break free and run away.

She heard the crew mutter various unkind things behind her back, and then they were there, walking alongside as she approached the automaton.

"Any advice, Dent?" Taj asked, hoping to take advantage of the AI's resource of knowledge in what she knew would be the toughest opponent she'd ever faced in her short life.

"Don't get hit," he suggested. "Try not to get stepped on either. It's hell on your posture."

Taj groaned and stared up at the automaton as it drew closer and closer, the ground rumbling at its approach.

She thought back on the crew's training sessions and how hard they'd prepared to be a part of the Federation and their teams, and here was the chance to show what all of them were made of and save lives in the process.

Taj sighed.

"It's hard being a hero sometimes," she told her crew. "Let's do this."

CHAPTER FOURTEEN

The giant automaton's fist slammed into the ground
right where Taj had stood only seconds before. Sand
flew in the air like a tiny eruption, and she darted around
the monster's hand, which was as wide across as she was
tall. The mechanoid beast drew his fist back quicker than
she could have imagined before she and the crew had
engaged the monster.

Now, it had sadly become what she expected, and she'd
learned to time its movements.

Taj bolted between the automaton's spread legs and
shot out behind it, giving herself a short break to catch her
breath as it tried to angle its mass and turn to follow her.

"This thing is killing us," Torbon called out. "Literally."

"Not yet," Taj muttered under her breath, but she knew
she was being spiteful. They were tiring fast, and Warpath
kept coming.

Cabe unloaded yet another magazine into the
automaton, this time at its ankle, trying to bring the giant

down. The weapon bursts scorched the metal and bounced away, digging pits in the sand where the ricochets hit.

Krawg hit it from the other side, stepping between its legs and shooting upwards into what could be considered its crotch.

"Is there someplace on this thing we haven't tried to shoot yet?" Cabe asked, circling the automaton to stay out of its line of sight as he reloaded, watching Krawg's shots reflect uselessly.

"Not that I can tell," Dent reported.

"Did we shoot it in its mouth yet?" Torbon asked, running over to them as Warpath spied one of the other warriors squirming injured in the dirt and went after him.

"Be right back," Taj announced and ran off, using the suit to push her as fast as she could go.

"Just that one time I hit it there by accident," Krawg answered. "Like everything else, it did nothing."

Warpath grabbed for the wounded man while the crew discussed the automaton, but Taj got there first, snatching him up and running off while the automaton got a handful of dirt for its effort. It roared its frustration at its lack of success. She dropped the warrior off a distance from the rest of the crew to try and keep him safe then returned to her people, panting.

"At least we're pissing it off," Lina said, clapping her hands. "That's something, right?"

"Oh, it's something, all right," Torbon replied, groaning as Warpath turned and headed in their direction again.

"We've got to figure something out, Taj," Cabe warned her. "Our guns can't stop it, our blades can't cut it, and we sure as gack can't punch the thing." He held up his broken hand as an example, the bones shattered and his fingers sitting crookedly as he tried to close it. "That didn't work out very well," he admitted.

"Who the gack tries to punch a metal giant?" Torbon wondered.

Lina subtly pointed a finger at Cabe, blocking it from his view with her other hand.

"Oh yeah," Torbon chuckled. "Cabe."

Warpath swung a backhand at the gathered mass of Furlorians, and they scattered ahead of it, each running a different direction to confuse the monster.

Of course, that really didn't do much seeing how it didn't have a real mind behind its actions. It was driven by pure instinct, a sub-level AI that would have struggled to run a hovercraft let alone anything more complex.

Still, it was completely relentless and never tired, and the Furlorians were the exact opposite.

They'd managed to keep most of the other warriors from dying so far, with one exception: a crazy fighter with a mohawk named Pao, who clearly had suicidal tendencies. Every time the crew dodged the automaton's left fist, they got to see Pao's last moments splattered across Warpath's massive knuckles.

"Poor Pao," Lina commented as she danced away. "He's starting to peel off now, at least."

The engineer had stopped even trying to shoot Warpath when it came at her, focusing all her remaining energy on avoiding his blows and finding someplace she could wait where she gained the most time in between attacks.

The crowd's excitement had waned since the match started. Where they'd been cheering and roaring at everything Warpath did, they'd long since grown tired of watching the Furlorians avoid the monstrosity and play babysitter to the other warriors.

Only Pao's passing had inspired a spurt of shouts and cries. After that, the crew had been met with a spattering of boos that reverberated throughout the arena on a regular basis. Taj knew those in charge of the fights would soon need to do something to end the bout before their monstrosity lost face with the crowd.

And just as she thought that, there was a surge of energy through the sand, and Warpath stiffened, stopping mid-step. Its armored skin gleamed and seemed to almost glow, energy flowing through it.

"Uh, what are they doing to it?" Taj asked Dent, wondering what the gack was going on.

Dent, for what was probably the tenth time, scanned the automaton. Whereas before, he stood stoic and announced he once again hadn't seen any appreciable weaknesses, this time his eyes went wide, eyebrows rising.

"That can't be good," Lina said, noticing Dent's reaction.

"I'm afraid it's not," he replied. "They're powering the automaton up."

"Which means what exactly?" Taj asked.

Dent stared at Warpath as its foot settled back on the sand and a tremble ran through it. "They just made it faster and stronger and likely more aggressive."

Torbon groaned. "Yeah, because it needed a boost in aggression. The thing's been trying to rip our heads off for twenty minutes now."

"Unsuccessfully," Lina corrected. "So far."

"If it makes you feel better, it's going to do it much

quicker now," Dent told him. "The ripping our heads off bit, that is. And pretty much everything else it does, too."

"Can't wait." Torbon glared at the monstrosity.

Warpath seemed to respond to him, raising its fists to the sky and howling. It sounded like a rocket launching. When it was done, it looked down and stormed toward the Furlorians again.

This time, it was much, much faster.

"Gack!" Taj mouthed as she leapt aside, barely avoiding the giant's blow this time around.

The rest of her crew had fared as well, but in her hurry, she hadn't noticed the warrior she'd saved earlier was still nearby.

Warpath snatched him up in a rush. The warrior screamed as the automaton lifted him into the air, massive fingers holding the man in place as if he were imprisoned.

Taj rolled out of her dive and willed her weapon out, but it was too late. Warpath squeezed.

There was a loud, wet *crunch*, and what was left of the warrior oozed out from between the automaton's gooey fingers.

Taj looked away, her stomach churning. She didn't even bother to shoot the thing. "That's gonna give me night-mares," she mumbled to herself.

"Heads up!" Lina shouted as Warpath charged at Taj again.

Taj faked left, then ran right, causing the automaton to stumble and nearly topple over as it missed its swipe at her.

"You see that?" Cabe called out.

"Super-charging the big guy makes him a bit clumsier, it looks like," Torbon said.

"Maybe we can take advantage of that," Taj told them. She glanced about and waved the Ursite over. "Krawg, with me."

Krawg growled. "I'm kind of wishing I'd got off the ship after I carried Dent in there," he spat out.

"And miss all this fun?" Torbon asked him.

"Our definitions of fun are radically different," he replied.

"Come on," Taj told him and ran off.

Krawg grunted and followed, despite all his complaining. "I hope you have a good plan," he said in between heavy huffs of breath.

"It's a plan," she replied, "but *good* is subjective."

"I'll save that phrase for use on your gravestone," Krawg said as they ran across the sand, circling behind Warpath.

Once they were there, Taj raised her gun and shot the automaton in the back of its head as it stomped after the other Furlorians.

It grumbled and spun, kicking up sand in its wake and barreling toward the pair.

"Was that the plan?" Krawg asked.

"The easy part," she replied, motioning for Krawg to stay right beside her. "The next bit is a little tricky."

"Let me guess," he said as the automation stormed toward them, "that's my part of the plan?"

"You catch on fast." Taj chuckled and angled herself just to the right of Warpath's foot as it came stomping down toward her.

As soon as it hit, Taj leapt backward over Krawg's head,

screaming, "Stay put! Don't move!" She fired dozens of rounds into the automaton's eyes as she did, blinding it for an instant.

"Sacrificing the Ursite is definitely not a good plan," he whined as Warpath raised its foot and launched forward to chase after Taj.

His giant sole loomed over Krawg's head, sand raining down on top of him.

"Trip him!" Taj shouted, hitting the ground and darting off once more to avoid Warpath's follow-up attack.

"For the record," Krawg stated as he reached out and latched onto Warpath's heel as it started to come down, "Dent specifically mentioned not to be stepped on, remember?"

The Ursite howled as he dug his fingers in as hard as he could and pulled with everything he had, leaning his full weight back as he did. Warpath dragged him along for about a meter before the automaton's forward momentum got the best of it. It grunted and reached out for Taj, who stayed within its reach, teasing it on.

"Come and get me!" she shouted, only darting off at the last minute as its fingers stretched out to grab her.

"Timber!" Torbon shouted from behind Krawg as he ran up and grabbed the Ursite by the belt, tugging him back as Krawg let go of the automaton's heel.

Warpath's center of gravity too far forward now, its arms extended and its torso jutting out, it toppled face-first into the sand, slamming into the ground with a bone-jarring *thud*.

A collective gasp rose from the crowd as Warpath hit.

The automaton thrashed and clawed, working to get its hand underneath itself.

"Have they done it?" the bearded announcer asked, his platform flying overhead. "Have these unknown warriors defeated the great and powerful Warpath?" he screamed.

"Have we?" Torbon asked, crossing his fingers that they had.

The crowd started to chant once more, "Warpath! Warpath! Warpath!"

"Ah, come on, people," Taj complained. "You can't cheer for the underdog for once?"

Warpath got his arms under him right then and pushed himself up to his knees and clearly looked around to find who'd tripped him. His steely gaze landed directly on Taj.

The crowd exploded.

"Guess not," Taj answered herself, seeing no one else was going to.

"He's...uh, getting back up," Krawg said, pointing to the automaton.

"You noticed that, huh?" Taj sniped, though her anger was at her leading them into the situation, not with the Ursite or his comment.

She turned to look at her crew and raised her hands questioningly. She was running out of ideas, not that she'd had a whole bunch of them to begin with. Taj was starting to think she might well need to abandon the rest of the warriors to their fate, as horrible as that would be.

She was already sick watching Pao and the other guy, whose name she never caught, get squished in front of her.

That's one gack of a eulogy, she thought. *Sorry, buddy.*

She glanced around the arena then, letting her eyes

scan the lights and the view screens as she looked for something she could use against the slowly rising automaton.

Her eyepiece zoomed in, Taj froze as she spotted someone in the crowd she recognized.

"You have got to be kidding me," she snarled.

"What?" Cabe asked, coming to stand alongside her, his broken hand dangling at his side.

"Is that who I think it is?" she asked, sending her eyepiece's signal to the others so they could see what see saw.

"Bloody Rowl!" Lina cursed, confirming that it was who Taj thought it was before anything else was even said.

"Our attacker from the caravan," Dent answered. "The one who tossed the grenade at the end."

Taj growled, zeroing in on the man she'd spied in the stands. He moved through the crowd slowly, glancing around in a manner that would have been suspicious had anyone been watching anything besides the giant monstrosity and its victims on the arena floor.

She spotted the scar that ran down his face and over his wayward eye as he moved along, and Taj seethed at seeing him. But as incensed as she was at seeing her attacker, alive and well and strolling along as if he hadn't a care in the world, what truly infuriated her was who she saw him walk right up to.

She ground her teeth together, her sharpened eyeteeth nicking her lower lip and drawing blood.

"That gackspittle worm!" she said with a growl.

Right there, in the stands in front of thousands of people, the man who'd attacked the crew's caravan walked directly up to the woman who'd abandoned them at that very same caravan: Commander Rolkar.

The scarred man stopped and leaned against the very railing she stared out from, less than a meter apart, and looked out over the spectacle.

Taj snarled at seeing them so close, doing their best to appear as if they had no clue the other stood right there while it was gacking obvious to Taj that the arrangement had been intentional. And though she couldn't see them communicating, she wondered if they had some form of internal communications like she and the crew did.

"What the gack are they doing here together?" she asked, making sure her eyepiece recorded everything.

"Might want to pay more attention to Warpath and less about Rolkar and her friend right now," Cabe warned as the automaton got to its feet and let loose a massive roar, swinging itself around so it could come after Taj and Krawg.

Taj was half-tempted to let the automaton smash her into dust while she took aim at the two backstabbers and blasted them where they sat conspiring.

It would be worth it.

Cabe apparently didn't think so.

He grabbed her and yanked her out of the way of Warpath's vengeful swipe for her head. The two rolled through the sand, kicking up golden dust in their wake. Taj stood up, her stare never once leaving the pair in the stands, acting as if each other were invisible.

A moment later, they both moved off, going their separate ways as if they'd never noticed one another.

"Oh no you don't," Taj snarled, trying to watch both of

them as they walked away in different directions.

"Incoming!" Dent called out.

Once more Cabe whipped her away from Warpath, its massive fist digging a hole in the sand where they'd been moments before.

"I get that you're angry, but I could really use your help right now or we're gonna get squished," Cabe pleaded, motioning toward the steel goliath who just kept marching toward them.

"Fine," she replied, snorting as she waved to Lina to get her attention, "but I'm not gonna let that scarred weasel off the hook."

"What do you need me to do?" the engineer asked, wisely keeping a safe distance.

Taj and Cabe leapt away from Warpath again, and Taj found her anger had given her just a hint of an edge, and she avoided the attack easily this time around.

"Move out of direct line of sight of the crowd and go camo-mode and follow after that little gackball," she told Lina. "The scarred one, obviously," she clarified. "We know where the other one will be at the end of the day."

"You sure?" Lina asked, then groaned when she'd realized what she'd done. "Sorry."

"Gacking right I'm sure," Taj answered, not even bothering to be annoyed by the question this time.

"What about you guys?" Lina asked as she hesitated to run off. "I don't want to leave you alone with that metal monstrosity."

"I have an idea," Taj answered.

"I hope it's a good one this time," Krawg called out as Warpath took a shot at him, the Ursite barely managing to slip away this time. He yipped as he lost some fur to the automaton's grasping hand.

"It is," she assured them both.

I hope.

She waved Lina off before she or anyone else could second guess her plan. Which was probably a good thing seeing how she hadn't completely figured it out yet, but the vague concept of it was running around in her head desperately trying to fully hatch.

Taj watched for a moment as Lina ran to the edge of the arena, then disappeared from view. She sighed, knowing that at least the engineer was free of the killing field for the moment, and she was glad of it.

Now, she needed to get the rest of them clear.

Krawg bounded away from Warpath and the automaton chased him, while Taj returned her attention to the lights and screens, wondering what she could bring down on the giant's metal head to slow him down or take him out.

The announcer flew by on his floating platform, and for a moment, Taj contemplated smashing him into Warpath, wondering if that would stop the behemoth or at least make its masters call their creature off to rescue the man before he got smashed.

And then it came to her.

She looked to the sky and grinned like a maniac.

"You're kind of scaring me," Cabe muttered beside her.

"It's not you who should be scared," she assured him.

Well, maybe a little, she thought. *We should probably all be a little scared right now.*

Taj willed her gun back to her hand and blasted

Warpath, drawing his attention to her once more and allowing Krawg to dart away.

"Did you really have to do that?" Cabe asked with a sigh.

She nodded. "We need to give Dent a couple of minutes to do something," she answered. "Follow along with me."

"I saw what you made Krawg do earlier," he argued. "I'm really not sure I want to go with you. Besides, I only have one hand." He held up his mangled hand and waved it in front of her.

"Just shut up and come on." She grabbed his other hand and ran off as Warpath charged at them, scooping up a handful of sand and flinging it about wildly in its fury, golden dust raining over them.

"Can you reach the other you aboard the ship?" Taj asked Dent.

"I can," he came back. "What do you want me to do?"

Taj and Cabe avoided Warpath once again and shot back between his legs, then reversed directions halfway through the maneuver and ran back the way they'd come. The automaton spun about and paused as it tried to determine where its targets had gone.

"Can you multi-task?" Taj asked the AI a second later.

Dent scoffed. "I'll have you know that I am—"

"A simple *yes* will suffice," she barked, no patience for his long-winded explanations as to his capabilities.

"Yes, I can multi-task," he answered, sighing. "No one appreciates the ability of a high-end AI such as myself," he complained, more to himself than anyone else, especially since no one was really listening.

"Good," Taj answered, "then this is what I need both of

you to do."

"We're both the same person, so you know," Dent told her.

She ignored him and explained what she needed of him while she and Cabe led Warpath on a merry chase, each blow getting closer as they tired more and more.

After several minutes of keeping the giant occupied, Cabe tripped and went down face-first into the sand. Taj skidded to a stop and darted back as Warpath grabbed at him. She blasted the automaton's hand and drew his attention once again, only this time she couldn't dart away.

His hand closed around her, and the behemoth howled its delight at having caught her at last.

Taj pushed her suit's defenses to their max to keep the automaton from crushing her into pulp. Fortunately, it wanted to lord its victory over her first, and Taj wondered if the thing really was entirely mechanical. It raised her in the air and showed his prize to the crowd who, of course, roared back at the beast, encouraging it to kill Taj.

Any time now would be perfect, she told Dent.

This isn't as easy as you'd think, he complained.

Scooping me up in a bucket after all this won't be easy either, she countered.

She spied Cabe as he got back to his feet and fired shot after shot into the automaton's spine, but the giant was content to ignore him and focus on Taj.

It leaned in close and leveled one eye directly in front of her so it could look right at her. Taj shuddered in its grip, but did her best to not show the monster any fear.

"You'll get what's coming to you," she told it, forcing an edge into her voice she didn't really feel.

Warpath seemed to chuckle, although Taj really wasn't sure what the sound was that it made, but it seemed amused nevertheless. It opened its mouth wide and moved to stuff her inside.

"Now would be good!" she screamed, scrambling to hang on to keep from being chewed up and swallowed by the steel beast.

Right then the lights all around the arena brightened, each of them giving off a whining hum as they grew brighter and brighter and brighter, blinding the audience and forcing them to turn away from the increasing brilliance.

People gasped and cried out as the lights gave way all at once, exploding and showering the crowd with sparks and tiny pieces of glass. The crowd ducked and turned away until the shower of debris subsided.

When they turned back, the only light illuminating the arena was that of the giant view screens. It took a moment for everyone's eyes to adjust, and then a gasp, even larger than the one that rang out just moments earlier, filled the air so loud it drowned out every other sound for an instant.

And there Taj stood, in the automaton's open, upright palm, pointing her pistol at Warpath's face.

A smoking crater sizzled right in the middle of Warpath's eyes, and the automaton seemed frozen in place as it came to terms with its sudden and unexpected demise.

The automaton dropped to a knee and teetered sideways. Taj rode it down, hopping from its hand as it struck the ground with a resounding *thud* that echoed through the silent arena.

A second later, the crowd erupted, screaming and howling and cheering so loud that the entire arena shook in response.

"They...they did...did it," the announcer muttered, appearing unable to wrap his tongue around the unthinkable.

"Gacking right we did," Taj said, walking over and joining the rest of her crew as the throng cheered all around them.

"We should probably go," Dent advised. "Before everyone realizes the shot that took out the automaton came from space and not from that tiny little blaster you're still clinging to."

Taj couldn't agree more. She led the crew to the shadows near the portcullis they'd entered through, aided by the lights Dent destroyed while blinding the crowd long enough to take out the automaton with the *Arrant's* one gun.

The old men at the gate triggered the mechanism that controlled the portcullis and stepped back wide-eyed as the crew marched through the opening and ran off, disappearing into the crowd and changing their appearance in rapid succession to confuse anyone watching. Once they broke free of the throng, they turned on their suits' camo-mode and vanished among the rooftops.

"I don't think you realize just how much control it takes to blast an automaton in the face with a ship's cannon and not kill everyone standing around it," Dent said as they ran.

Taj sighed. "Someone pat him on the back before he breaks his arm trying to do it himself."

CHAPTER FIFTEEN

Skol Arduin washed Grom's blood from his hands and returned to his chambers, frustrated that he had failed to make Grom crack, as had Vetrus before him. He returned to his seat, wringing his hands as they dried.

Grom Hadar had turned out to be far more difficult than Skol had imagined. Though Skol had known little of his background, he couldn't have pictured the man withstanding both his and Vetrus's attention, yet here he was, defying them both no matter how much blood he shed in the process.

It was infuriating.

His master's patience was finite and time was running out, both for Alshan Ra's plans and for Skol's efforts.

The appearance of what Skol believed to be Etheric Federation operatives had thrown the organization into chaos despite the short time the Furlorians had been on-planet. The failed attempts to kidnap them were black eyes on Skol's efforts.

He'd sent the scarred puppet, Blas, out to make contact with Alshan Ra, so perhaps the pair could coordinate and produce something more akin to success, but the master had been reluctant to get personally involved as doing so might compromise his ultimate goal.

A goal that relied on Skol's assurances that no outsiders, especially the Federation, would interfere with his plans.

Unfortunately, Skol had failed to keep up his part of the bargain so far.

"He's here," Vetrus told him from the doorway, interrupting Skol's disappointed reverie.

Skol groaned under his breath, waving the man on despite his reluctance. "Send him in, Vetrus."

It wasn't Alshan Ra himself, of course, as it never was, but Skol knew well enough that Blas's return, given Skol's list of failures, was not a good sign.

Alshan Ra's would-be harbinger of doom was a pathetic creature.

He shuffled in quietly, head down and staring at the floor with his three good eyes. The fourth, ever wayward, glared up at Skol, red and angry and full of a malevolence its master was never capable of.

In this instance, however, Skol felt a chill skitter up his spine at seeing that scarred eye.

Blas came over and stood before Skol's chair, and Skol wished he had killed the man the last time he stood there. It would have been an easy thing.

Blas was nothing, a zealot whose usefulness had long gone the way of his wandering eye. Still, Skol couldn't help but realize just how different the man's return was compared to when Skol had first sent him away and spared his life.

Blas held his silence until, at last, Skol urged him to speak.

"Tell me, Blas, did you do as I asked?"

"I did, of course," he answered, delivering his answer with far more confidence than Skol had expected.

Despite it all, there was a definite tremor in his hands as he held them to his sides. Skol took solace in that.

"I spoke with the master's emissary. Alshan Ra feels it is time to move forward with his plans, regardless of your... uh, failed efforts—his words, forgive me—regarding the Federation agents. He has set things in motion."

Skol resisted the urge to jump to his feet and butcher Blas where he stood. His fury roiled in his belly, and he leaned forward to put pressure on it, to contain it as he hunched over on himself.

He's nothing, Skol told himself over and over in his head. *He's a messenger, nothing more.*

"Tell me, Blas," Skol asked, "does the master have any orders for me in light of this revelation regarding my...failure?"

Both Skol and Blas knew Blas would not live long enough to convey Skol's attitude to their mutual master, so while Blas might feel strong enough to pass on Alshan Ra's words verbatim, he knew they were no shield for Skol's inevitable wrath.

"He...he would speak with you in...in person," Blas answered, braving the barest of glances up at Skol as if he knew the man's thoughts about diving on top of him and slitting his throat.

Skol sighed. "He would, would he?"

Blas nodded. "I was told to collect you," he managed to spit out. "Time is of the essence, as it was explained to me."

"That it most assuredly is, Blas," Skol said, rising to his feet. "That it is."

He had the slightest flicker of satisfaction when he saw Blas flinch at his sudden movement, but the joy was fleeting.

Much like his patience, Alshan Ra was not known for his mercy. As long as there was a distance between Skol and his master, there was a sense of security, however tenuous, but it was there, and Skol reveled in it. It was the buffer between his world and Alshan Ra's.

Each was the master of their own domain, and the lines of power rarely crossed. But when they did, like now, it was a sickening reminder to Skol just how delicate the balance was. Here in his world, Skol was king. He did as he wished, slept soundly and without remorse, and spent his days enjoying the moments he had.

However, with Alshan Ra's invitation hanging in the air, the balance had been grievously upset. Now, though Blas was simply too dense to ever realize it, the *invitation* he'd extended to Skol changed everything.

With those few words uttered by an idiot tongue, Alshan Ra had debased Skol, pulled him from the top of the world and tugged him eye-level with Blas, kicking and screaming the entire way down.

In that moment, Skol was no better than Blas.

They were both puppets, pets to be kicked and discarded at the whims of their master.

Like Blas, Skol was *nothing*.

He sighed low enough that Blas would not hear him, and Skol left his chair behind to stand before the cowering Blas. He stared at the retch before him and, again, thought back to when he might have killed the man for his failure.

But what difference would it make beyond a fleeting moment of satisfaction?

If he had nothing left to him, Skol would at least clasp the certainty that, if nothing else, he held Blas's fate in his hand in a way that Blas would never hold his.

Skol reached out and patted Blas on the shoulder, grinning as the man flinched at his touch.

"Take me to the master, Blas. I'm ready."

Blas shuffled back and turned on his heel awkwardly, marching toward the open door where Vetrus stood vigil.

"I'm off to see Alshan Ra," Skol told his right-hand man as he followed Blas toward the door. "You're in charge while I'm away. Make the most of it," he said before he left.

Vetrus chuckled in reply.

Unlike Blas, Vetrus knew exactly what his value was.

You were on top of the hill until you weren't, someone dragging you down kicking and screaming the entire way.

And then you were gone.

Skol followed Blas out onto the street, motioning for several of the guards stationed there to follow him.

He knew what was coming and could accept it...to a point.

Skol would play his role unless there was an opportunity to change it.

He would kick and scream as he was pulled down the hill, but he would never surrender.

CHAPTER SIXTEEN

The crew caught up to Lina outside of a small, rundown building in the heart of the Dulta ghetto.

"You're certain this is where he went?" Taj asked the engineer.

"Absolutely," she answered. "He wasn't exactly difficult to follow, you know." Lina glanced around at the crew, taking them all in for a moment as they sat there, staring at the building. "By the way, how did you all escape the arena? You never did say."

"You can ask Dent about that later," Taj told her. "I'm sure he'll be glad to tell you all about it...at length."

The AI huffed. "While it might not have been my idea, I played my part admirably," he grumbled, clearly disappointed he wasn't being allowed to brag adequately.

Cabe held up his wounded hand and winked at Lina. "One solid punch from me was all it took," he told her.

Lina chuckled. "I was there when you broke it, genius,"

she replied. "That's all it took to make you whimper like a kitten."

"Oh yeah." Cabe sniffed. "Well, it *did* hurt."

Lina patted his shoulder sympathetically. "Your ego most of all, I'm sure."

"There sure are a lot of guards around," Taj muttered, mostly to herself as she kept watch on the squat, rundown building Lina had followed the scarred grenadier to after he'd left the arena.

The thought of seeing him and Commander Rolkar so close and acting as if they didn't know each other was infuriating after everything that had happened. That woman had been right on top of them from the start of the mission, and though Taj had her suspicions early on, she'd still let Rolkar manipulate them and put her people at risk.

The first chance Taj got, she would make Rolkar pay for that. She had no doubt the woman was the reason Grom had disappeared. She was working with the zealots and had to have sold Grom out to them, just like she'd tried to sell the crew out to the hooded man and his disciples when they'd first arrived.

That was something she couldn't forgive.

Taj shifted uncomfortably as her thoughts raged. She wanted to rush into the building and confront the scarred man and those he worked for. While they hadn't been able to ascertain who else was in the building with the would-be assassin, Taj didn't care.

She could picture him in there alongside more of his zealot brothers and likely even their master, the mysterious man in the hood Dent had yet to find any reference of in recent news.

She wanted to kick down the door and start shooting, blast them all and sort the carnage out afterward, like the zealots had tried to do with the caravan.

Taj caught herself feeling antsy, her gun in her hand though she couldn't remember willing it there, and she stood on the edge of the rooftop, far closer than she should be to avoid being spotted. Her hand ached around the grip of her pistol.

Fortunately, the guards shuffled about just then as if on some unseen cue, and the door to the building opened. Taj remembered her place and stepped back, letting her suit's camo-program do its job.

She realized just how close she'd come to letting her anger overtake her, and she sighed.

All she'd been through—what they'd all been through— had changed her, she knew. She wasn't that innocent child she'd been back on Krawlas before the invasion of the Wyyvan.

She'd seen too much since then, experienced too much. And now, she'd been given an opportunity to do more than be a victim, a survivor. While hardly a world-beater in the larger scheme of things, Taj understood she had more power now than she'd ever possessed in her entire existence. She could make a difference, not only in her life, but in those of the people around her. She could help others like she was trying to do with Grom Hadar.

Cabe set a hand on her shoulder, and Taj clasped it in hers, offering him a slight smile.

And she wasn't alone.

Taj drew a deep breath and brought her emotions under control. She'd been scared not too long ago, weak and unsure of herself. And now she was strong and had the means to fight back, yet she was still unsure.

She needed to find the balance, the line between being the person she used to be and the person the world had made her into.

Taj had to be both, had to straddle that line to be the best version of herself that she could be.

And she would, she promised herself.

"You okay?" Cabe asked, leaning over her shoulder.

She nodded. "I'm great," she told him, giving him a quick kiss simply because she wanted to, not because she needed to distract or shut him up.

"Who's that?" Lina asked as another man strolled out of the building behind the scarred one.

Taj inched closer to the edge and zeroed in on the man Lina pointed out.

"I have no idea," Taj answered, shrugging, "but he looks to be in charge."

The man, who walked with an ease that spoke of his confidence, waved at the guards and all but two of the ten stationed in front of the building trailed off after him.

He wasn't dressed in robes like the scarred one, but rather in a casual outfit of black shirt and pants and calf-high boots. His hair was slick and dark, and the men he'd commanded made it clear they were there for him, not the scarred one.

The grenadier marched ahead of the group, like a pet given a little bit of an extra leash. His chin hung toward the ground as he walked, his hands hanging limp at his sides.

Taj immediately pictured a man condemned and imagined he was what one would look like.

"I'm not picking this man's face up in my scans either," Dent informed the group. "I must not be digging far enough back or these men, this one and the hooded man, have done an excellent job of staying out of the spotlight."

Taj sighed. She'd been hoping following the scarred zealot would lead to some big revelation. So far, they were nearly as much in the dark as they had been when they first arrived.

"What do we do?" Torbon asked. "Do we follow these guys?"

Taj made a decision right then.

"Yes," she answered, pointing to Torbon, Lina, Cabe, and Krawg in turn. "You four, follow them and see where they go, but don't engage them unless you absolutely have to. I don't want anyone getting hurt."

"What are you gonna do?" Cabe asked, clearly realizing she had something in mind for her and Dent.

"We're gonna go inside and see what we can find here," she told him.

"I don't like this," he replied.

"Me either," Lina said, shaking her head. "Splitting up's not a good idea."

Krawg chuckled. "She's not exactly known for good ideas, though, is she?"

The crew turned to glare at the Ursite as he grinned and raised his hands to ward them off.

"He's right, you know," Dent told her with his usual bluntness. "I mean, they get there and things would work out, certainly, but I would have a hard time categorizing any of your plans as *good*. I'm sure the crew agrees."

Lina, Cabe, and Torbon all turned their glare toward Dent.

"Am I wrong?" he asked.

None of the crew answered him.

Taj chuckled at their reluctance. "I never said this was a good idea." She poked a playful finger Krawg's direction before looking back at the rest. "But it's something we need to do," she told them. "We have no idea where Grom is, but his disappearance has to be connected to these people somehow. The only way we're gonna do that is if we take a look inside this place."

"But to split us up like this…" Cabe started. "Did you see how many guards that guy took with him? How many do you think are still in there if he can afford to have so many escort him?"

"Probably way less for exactly that reason, Cabe," she argued. "I'm expecting resistance, of course, but that guy looked like the boss, right?"

She didn't give them time to answer before she went on.

"That means he is gonna have the bigger entourage than anyone he leaves behind."

"Logic is not your friend, it seems," Dent told her.

"Well, it sort of makes sense," Torbon said. "I can see it when you put it like that, yeah."

"Thus proving my point," Dent replied.

"Hey!" Torbon complained, suddenly realizing what the AI meant.

Taj waved them all to silence. "It's not a discussion, guys," she told them. "We need to both search this place and follow those two. Because there are so many of them, I want to be sure there are enough of you should something go wrong and you need to fight." She motioned to the building across the way. "Dent and I can handle whatever's in there." She reached out and patted Dent on the shoulder proudly. "Dent is the one who took out Warpath, remember?"

"All manipulative efforts at trying to get me to agree with her aside," Dent said, "I believe Taj is correct about this course of action." He winked at her, not even bothering to try and hide it from the others.

"You suck at subterfuge," Taj told him. Then before the others could start arguing again, she leaned in and kissed Cabe hard on the mouth. "Go before you guys lose them," she said, pushing him back gently.

"There you go," Torbon muttered. "The kiss of death has been invoked. Cabe has lost all ability to reason, so let's just go do this."

Lina chuckled and started off, Torbon alongside her. Krawg grunted and followed after, snapping his fingers for Cabe to follow along. Cabe sighed after a moment's indecision and spun around, jogging to catch up with the others.

"Why does that always work?" Taj heard him ask as they leapt off the building and went in pursuit of the scarred zealot and the man with him.

Taj blushed at hearing Torbon's answer drift to her across the comm.

Dent chuckled. "On that note, how about we assault a building?"

"Gladly," Taj answered, letting her mask come up over her face to hide her embarrassment.

She drew in a deep breath, waited until the two guards at the door looked away, then signaled for Dent to move.

The pair of them leapt off the edge of the building and sailed straight toward the pair of guards. Before either knew what was happening, Taj had clobbered the first of the men, and Dent had knocked the second out with a downward angled blow.

Both guards crumpled to the ground in contorted heaps.

"Should we just leave them here?" Dent asked.

Taj shook her head. "I learned from the last time, believe it or not." She grabbed her man and returned to the building they'd just jumped off, then tossed the unconscious guard onto the roof.

"Again, logic is not your strong suit," Dent argued, following her example.

Taj grinned. "Who needs logic when you have powered armor?"

"Both are best," he answered.

She shrugged. "Maybe, but we'll have to agree to disagree," she said as she went over to the door and examined it, realizing it was unlocked when she went to test the handle.

"That's convenient," she said, easing the door open.

"It likely means whoever is here is deemed sufficient for the defense of this place or they would have secured it better," Dent countered, pointing at Taj with an *aha* face. "Now that is logic in action."

"No, that's just like...your opinion," she told him, walking inside without another word.

"You realize, of course, that I can't have the ship fire its gun on a building to rescue us should something bad occur this time, right?" Dent said to her back before joining her.

Taj didn't bother to reply.

She crept through the hall with her gun drawn, wondering just what they might run into inside the old building.

A narrow hallway stretched out a short distance before them, and there were two doors off to each side before the hall terminated and led out into what appeared to be a large room, though Taj could only see a small portion of it from her position. A pair of view screens were partially visible on the far wall, though both were black and lifeless.

Other than that, there was nothing to be seen.

Both Dent and she crept to the edge of the open doors in the hall and glanced inside. Taj's room, a tiny office-looking space, was empty, nothing more than a small desk with a folding chair set behind it.

Dent's room, however, appeared to have an occupant.

"Hey!" a man shouted in a surprised voice.

And then there was a meaty *thud*, and the man grunted in pain. One last *thud* rounded out the series, and Taj turned around in time to see the man slump over a desk similar to the one in the opposite room.

"See?" Taj said. "Who needs spaceship guns when you have fists?"

"Again, both are always nice."

This time, she agreed with a nod. Both *were* nice.

The pair crept to the edge of the hall, and Taj peeked around the corner. She'd been right. The room was large, a singular open space that likely took up the vast majority of the building's floor plan.

Across from the view screens mounted on the wall, there was a worn but comfortable-looking chair that looked as if it got plenty of use. It sat upon a short dais that might more appropriately be called a step. It didn't raise the chair high off the floor, but it still gave enough of the impression that it was intended for someone of stature.

Taj presumed it belonged to the man who'd left with the zealot.

Not seeing anyone in the room, she stepped inside and moved toward an open door that loomed to her left. To the right, the room stretched on, and there was what appeared to be an elevator on that side.

That part of the room was dark and gloomy, but her eyepiece made it easy to see, just as it had with the smoke when the caravan had been attacked.

Once more, Taj marveled at the technology Dent had been able to supply them with, thanks to the Federation's help.

"We've company," Dent said over the comm.

Where? she asked, using the mental link instinctively, forgetting that her voice wouldn't carry outside of the suit's mask without her wanting it to.

Dent pointed with his gun as a handful of men walked into the room from the open door she'd been moving to inspect. They drew and raised their weapons in response, causing a bit of a standoff.

Taj eased to her right a little and followed suit, aiming her gun at the men.

"This is unfortunate," the man in the middle of the group said. His voice sounded as if he was gargling shards of glass.

Taj found herself wondering what had happened to him to make him sound that way. She glanced at his throat but saw no indication of a wound that might be the cause.

"We weren't expecting company," the man went on. "We'll have to see you out, I'm afraid." He motioned with the gun toward the exit, but it was clear to Taj he would gladly shoot them in the back the second they turned around.

The broad, pleasant smile on his face never reached his eyes. They stared back cold and devoid of feeling, and Taj felt as if the man was staring right through her.

"Who are you?" she asked.

"You don't get to ask questions," he told her matter-of-factly, the veneer slipping slightly. "Please, the door, if you will." He motioned toward the exit with his gun once more.

That was when Taj spied the red staining his hand.

She focused in with her eyepiece and the suit's scanners confirmed her suspicions. It was blood.

"Hurt anyone nice lately?" Taj asked flippantly, knowing damn well that he had.

The man's lower set of eyes narrowed, but Taj had seen enough to decide on her course of action.

She would shoot first and ask questions later.

Except she'd actually shot second and asked a question first, but she was still quicker on the draw.

She tapped the trigger and blasted the raw-throated man in the hand that held his weapon. He shrieked and stumbled back, clutching his wounded fingers, and his gun clattered to the floor.

Everyone else opened fire then.

Taj caught a blast against her armor and grunted as it

took the brunt easily enough. It still hurt, but it hadn't penetrated.

Dent shot down two of the men in rapid succession by spraying shots from left to right, his android reflexes hitting the trigger so quickly so that his finger was a blur of motion.

Taj dodged a second shot from the man who'd hit her the first time around and retaliated, shooting him dead center in the face.

With no helmet to protect him, he flopped to the ground with a smoking crater in his head.

Dent shot the last of the men, killing him before he had time to do anything but graze Dent with his own gunfire. Before the man collapsed, Dent ran over to the group and aimed his pistol at the raw-throated man who'd threatened them

Taj came over and kicked his gun away from him, listening as it skittered across the floor and thumped into the distant wall.

"You see his hands?" Taj asked the AI.

Dent nodded, inching forward with his gun barrel leading the way. "Where's the blood from?"

"Do you think you scare me?" he asked in reply.

"We should," Taj said, letting her weapon slip back into the suit and hunkering down in front of the man.

She made the suit peel away from the tips of her fingers on one hand and rested her palm on his cheek, her sharp claws hovering just in front of two of his eyes.

Hold him, she told the AI.

The man swallowed hard and tried to flinch away, but

Dent reached over and wrapped his free hand around the back of the man's neck, holding him in place.

"Where's the blood from?" Taj asked again, letting a hint of fire slip into her tone. She fought to keep her hand from trembling.

The man glared at her for a long moment, seeming to question her willingness to back up her threat, but when she eased forward and scraped his eyelid with the tip of her claw, drawing a dot of blood that ran over his eyelashes, he acquiesced.

"There's a captive downstairs," he said in his raw voice, glancing toward the elevator. "That's where the blood is from."

"See, that wasn't too hard, was it?" Taj asked. "Who's the captive?" she asked, but she had a pretty good idea as to who it was already.

The man swallowed once more, a hint of defiance in his eyes, but he'd already given up the important information. Taj could tell he was stalling simply to make himself feel better about his situation.

"Grom Hadar," he answered, spitting out the name.

Taj fought back the urge to sigh at hearing the man's name. Instead, she forced a growl out, her whiskers fluttering in the man's face.

"If you've hurt him..." she started, an inner voice telling her how stupid that sounded given that the man had just admitted the blood on his hands was Grom's. Of course he'd hurt him.

Taj whipped back her arm and howled. The man screamed as her claws raked towards his face, but Dent held him still.

Then, at the very last moment, she clenched her fist and punched the man in the jaw.

There was a brittle crack, like twigs snapping, and the man slumped into Dent's hand. The AI let the man go a second later, and he flopped to the ground, his head thudding on the cold concrete.

"I thought for a second there you were actually going to take his eyes," Dent admitted, looking at Taj.

She drew in a deep breath and forced a smile onto her lips. "Me too," she told him.

The pair stood there staring at each other for a moment before Taj turned away and started across the room toward the elevator. Dent trailed along, dragging the man's unconscious body behind him.

Taj glanced over her shoulder at him, raising an eyebrow and wondering what he was doing.

"I presume the mechanism to operate the elevator is bio-oriented based on that scanner alongside the door," he answered without her having to actually ask the question. "And I figure this is easier, and far less messy, than lopping off his hand or trying to hack the system."

"That's that logic stuff again, isn't it?" she asked with a grin.

"It is indeed."

CHAPTER SEVENTEEN

Lina and the others followed the two men and their entourage of guards to another area of town, and while it appeared slightly more maintained and less weathered than the last location, there was nothing that made it feel as if the group were just out for a lovely stroll.

The two men knocked on the door of a squat, thick building that took up most of the block. A man in a black robe opened it and invited them in. The fur on the back of Lina's neck stood up as she watched from her perch across the road. The squadron of guards remained outside, taking up stations.

"Guess that confirms they're all connected then," Krawg said, having spied the zealot at the door.

Lina nodded. "Looks that way."

"Wonder what they're doing here?" Torbon asked, settling in to get comfortable, obviously presuming they were in for a long wait like at all the other locations.

"Could be anything," Lina answered.

"But nothing good," Cabe corrected.

Lina couldn't help but agree with that assessment. Nothing had been *good* since they'd arrived.

"I wish I knew what was going on," the engineer mused. "It's like having a game board with all these moving pieces floating around and not knowing any of the rules. It's frustrating."

"That's when you say 'gack it' and cheat," Torbon replied, grinning.

Krawg chuckled. "And how exactly do you intend to do that?"

Torbon rubbed his chin, thinking. "Well, first, I'd—"

"Find food?" Cabe cut in.

Torbon broke into a broad grin. "You know me so well."

"I could get behind that plan," Krawg agreed, nodding at Torbon.

"Doesn't look like you're gonna get the chance," Lina told him, tapping Torbon in the ribs and pointing at movement across the street. "Unless of course any of these guys are planning on bringing us over some takeout."

The crew crept closer to the edge and looked out over the street below. Krawg grunted, and Cabe mimicked him, obviously agreeing with the sentiment, whatever it was.

"Zealots," Cabe announced unnecessarily. They all knew what they were. The problem was how many of them there happened to be.

At first, just a few men stepped outside and milled among the guards, then two more joined them, and the building seemed to spit them out as if it was manufacturing them.

Ten, fifteen, twenty-five, forty men walked out of the

building in rapid succession. It looked like a convention at a robe factory, Lina thought, staring down at the group who stood silently, not saying so much as a word to one another or to the guards they had essentially swallowed whole into their midst.

"That's a whole lot of zealots," Torbon muttered.

Lina definitely agreed with that assessment as she looked over the crowd. She spotted the scarred one among their ranks, grateful to at least know where one of the men were right then. The guards that had come with him began a push toward each other, apparently feeling uncomfortable among so many of the zealots.

"They don't have their hoods on, though," Cabe mentioned. "That must be a good thing, right?"

Lina didn't think it was.

"Why are they just sitting there?" Krawg asked, scratching at the matted fur on his cheek.

As if in answer, several more zealots came out of the building and joined the rest. Once they were there, the men offered what looked like reassuring nods to those gathered closest.

The crowd of zealots sang a word aloud, each in tune and in perfect harmony, and then there was a flash of steel.

"What the gack?" Torbon shouted over the comm.

Lina felt as if she were going to be sick.

Down below, the mass of zealots turned on the guards, pulling knives and driving them down into the unsuspecting guards over and over again.

It happened so fast that it was over before Lina and the crew could really even process it.

"They...they killed them all," Cabe mouthed, barely able to catch his breath and spit the words out.

The whole group of zealots started off like a herd that had been spooked.

They split into groups and circled around the nearby buildings, splitting apart even more and spilling out into the streets, hiding their weapons as they went. All of them headed in the same general direction yet all choosing to take a different route to get there, and not one of them looking back at the pile of bodies they'd left in their wake.

Lina struggled to breathe and caught sight of a flash of metal reflected from one of the stragglers, the last man to leave the house, and she focused in on him to keep from seeing the blood spilling across the road.

The zealot stepped around a corner to be out of sight of the street and lifted up his robes. Lina readied to look away, thinking distractedly that she was about to witness a man urinating, when she realized he had clothes on underneath the robes.

But that wasn't all he had.

There was a wide belt wrapped around his waist, a number of wires looped underneath what looked like full pockets in the belt. The man tugged a loose wire up, apparently what Lina had seen reflecting the sun, and hooked it to one of the pockets.

Her breath caught in her lungs as she realized what the man had just done and what he was wearing.

"Oh...gack!" she mumbled as the man lowered his robes and scuttled off to follow the rest of the strolling zealots. She swayed at the revelation and stuck a hand on the ledge to hold herself steady.

"What is it?" Torbon asked, coming over to her to check if she was okay. "What's wrong now?"

"We are so gacked," she muttered, staring off after the zealots.

"Why is everyone stealing my line?" Torbon complained halfheartedly, clearly not wanting to process what they'd just witnessed.

Cabe came over and grabbed Lina by the shoulder. "What's going on? Uh, I mean, besides all that down there."

She shrugged him off and plopped down on the rooftop, drawing her view screen out of her suit. Her fingers flew across the keypad as she accessed Dent's network and started poring through it.

"Are you gonna tell us, or what?" Torbon asked, growing impatient. "Things are getting out of hand."

"Oh…" she let out, looking up with wide eyes. "We've got trouble. *Big* trouble."

"You mean bigger trouble than a bunch of guys stabbing a bunch of other guys?" Torbon asked.

Lina ignored his pleas for clarification and jumped on the comm.

"Taj, Dent," she called out. "We've got a serious issue out here," she told them. "The zealots are on the move. They've killed a bunch of men and they've got explosives!"

"Explosives?" Cabe asked, snapping about and looking over the ledge to where most of the zealots were still visible a short way off in the distance.

"You mean bombs?" Torbon asked for clarification. "These guys have bombs strapped to them on top of the damn knives? What happens if those things go off?"

Krawg raised both hands in the air and said, "Boom!"

Dent and Taj rode the elevator down in silence.

The trick of using Vetrus's hand—which was what the bio-scanner announced his name to be—worked perfectly. Dent dragged the unconscious man along with them, just in case they needed to use his biometrics to bring the elevator back up.

Two floors down, the elevator *dinged* and the doors opened. Taj stepped out ready to fight, expecting a mass of guards to be there waiting on them, but there was no one there. Just a short, empty hallway that ended at a thick, steel door. Several more doors lined the sides of the hall.

The smell of mildew struck her right away as she stepped off the elevator. The air was cold and crisp, especially compared to the warm air upstairs.

Dent motioned toward the far door with his eyes, and Taj spied another biometric scanner there.

"Logic, yes, I know," she told the AI.

"It might rub off on you yet," he replied.

The pair crept down the hall and examined the doors to the side and discarded them, the bio-scanners covered in ages of dust that made it clear none of them had been used any time recently.

The one at the end, however, had been wiped clean.

Dent raised Vetrus's hand and set the palm against the plate. The magnetic lock clicked, and Taj eased the door open, leading the way with her pistol out.

She put her gun away an instant later when she saw what was inside.

Taj hissed and raced into the cell.

"I'll stay here with this fellow," Dent said, watching the unconscious man as well as keeping an eye on Taj should she need assistance.

"Grom," Taj shouted, running over to the battered man curled up in the corner of the tiny cell. She hunkered down beside him and checked his vitals with her eyepiece, doing a quick scan.

"He's alive," she said softly, "but only just barely."

He looked like gack.

Grom Hadar had clearly been tortured, beaten so close to death that Taj was afraid to move him, but she didn't have a choice. She eased him over and cradled him in her arms, calling his name over and over in hopes of rousing him.

She was partially successful.

His four eyes fluttered, but only one seemed to look straight at her. The rest rolled about without control.

"Can you hear me?" she asked.

His only response was a flutter of his eyelids.

She pressed on. "We're from the Etheric Federation," she told him. "We're here to rescue you."

Hearing that, he groaned and tried to sit up. Taj held him still so he wouldn't hurt himself further.

"Don't move," she said. "We'll get you out of here, just hang on."

Grom mumbled something Taj couldn't hear, so she leaned in closer, ignoring the dots of spittle that peppered her fur as he tried to speak.

"T-th-e qu-quee-n," he finally managed, and Taj couldn't help but admire the man's tenacity.

"I know," she told him, doing her best to reassure the

wounded man. "We've seen the photos and heard the hooded-man's speeches. We know the queen's in danger, and as soon as we get you off-planet, we'll be sure to warn her."

Grom gurgled and did his best to shake his head. "N-n-no. M-mus-t-t s-sta-y."

Taj narrowed her eyes as she tried to decipher what he meant. "Stay here." She pointed to the cell.

His head wobbled side to side. "D-d-dult-a," he spat out finally.

"I think he wants to remain in the city," Dent clarified.

"I got that," Taj snarled. "But why?" she asked.

Grom summoned a surge of strength and managed to sit up in her arms, his entire body trembling at the effort.

"B-br-r-o-ther," he told her, and Taj had to lean in close to be sure she heard him properly.

"Brother?"

Grom nodded and slumped into her arms, lapsing into unconsciousness again.

"He has a brother here?" Taj asked Dent.

The AI shrugged. "I'm scanning the databases for information," he answered. "The Federation didn't provide us any familial connections and we didn't think to ask. It wasn't pertinent to the mission."

Taj growled. "It apparently is now."

She eased up, getting to her feet and carrying Grom with her, making sure she didn't jostle him too much.

"Let's get him someplace safe we can look him over, then we figure out whatever this gack is about his brother." Taj bit back another growl, realizing that no amount of complaining was going to make anything better.

Dent used Vetrus's hand one last time to open the elevator doors and booted him down the hall with swift kick.

Taj glanced over at the AI. "Why you leaving him behind?"

"He's a bit of a drag," he answered with a straight face.

"Seriously?" Taj laughed under her breath, unable to help herself despite how bad the attempted joke was.

The two rode up the elevator like they'd ridden it down: in silence.

Mostly.

Taj broke out into random chuckles every time she thought of Dent's joke.

Once the reached the top floor, the two of them slipped out of the building, Taj still lugging Grom along.

"The zealots are on the move. They've killed a bunch of men and they've got explosives!" Lina's voice shrieked across the comm the minute they stepped out into bright daylight.

"Wait!" Taj exclaimed. The words, while she'd understood them, didn't make any sense. "What do you mean explosives?"

Lina came back, "They're strapped with bombs, Taj. Probably all of them. They're moving off in a group of forty or more. They killed all the men that escorted the two we were following."

"Oh...Rowl," Taj muttered, glancing over at Dent wide-eyed and trembling. She could imagine—and she didn't want to—what these zealots were planning. There was no way it could end well, especially since it had started with blood already.

"Where are they headed?" Dent asked, giving Taj a moment to catch her breath and process the information.

"I think they're headed for the palace," Lina replied. "I scanned all the local news channels and databases and it looks as if Queen Rilan is holding a celebratory gathering of some sort for a sibling returning to the planet after being gone since they were kids or something."

Taj stiffened at hearing that. "A public celebration?"

Lina came back breathless, "A huge one, Taj. It's being held at the—"

"The palatial courtyards," Dent finished, having apparently researched the information while Lina was talking. "There will be thousands of people in attendance."

"Gack it!" Taj cursed. "Follow them, Lina. Follow them and stop as many of them as you can. We'll meet you there soon. Out," she shouted.

"I'll reach out to security services anonymously and see if I can rally them," Dent said, though Taj could tell from the look on his face that he didn't think there was much hope of that.

Them being outlaws made it even harder to contact the palace and tell them what was happening. By the time they managed to clear their name enough to get the whole story out, whatever plot the zealots were masterminding would be long over.

"Maybe reach out to Zel, if you're able," she added. "He might be able to warn Queen Rilan quickly enough."

Dent nodded, doing both apparently inside his head where Taj couldn't hear.

Taj glanced down at Grom and shook her head. She'd

almost forgotten him in all the craziness. "We can't take him with us. He won't make it."

Dent agreed. "Then we drop him off at his hideout," he said, starting off without waiting for Taj's confirmation.

She chased after him, able to do nothing else. "What about—"

"I've checked Lina's bug feeds," he answered before she even got the whole question out. "The room is clear. No one's been there since we last departed."

Taj nodded, though Dent wasn't looking at her to see it, and followed. Though she'd wanted to take to the roofs to keep from being spotted by any roving Heltrol or zealots, she knew Grom couldn't handle the extra stress that kind of travel would put on his body. So instead, she hunkered down and ran as smoothly as she could to keep from jarring him over-much, avoiding eye contact with anyone they came across.

After what seemed to be forever, they returned to Grom's hideout and slipped inside unseen. Taj went over and laid him gently on the couch, pulling the blanket up over him and setting the pillow under his head.

She listened to his breathing for a second, and the only good thing she could take away from that was that he was breathing at all. He took short, shallow breaths in rapid succession, and his body twitched every time he exhaled.

"He doesn't look good," Taj said, frustrated that they hadn't been better prepared for all the possibilities. With no medical gear on them, there was nothing she could do to try and stabilize the man

"This will have to do, Taj," Dent told her. "Security services have rerouted my call a couple hundred times or more trying to trace it. They're not taking me seriously, as I feared they wouldn't."

Taj rose to her feet and looked at Grom one last time, wishing him the best. She ran a hand over his forehead, daring a prayer to Rowl and hoping she hadn't made things worse by doing so.

Still, there was nothing else she could do for him right then. He had to make it through on his own if he was going to make it at all.

"Then it's up to us," Taj said, turning her back on Grom, for what she hoped was not the last time, and headed for the door. Dent followed.

Time was running out and people were going to die if they didn't do something.

What that something was, she had no idea, but she gack well was going to do something.

She had to, simple as that.

CHAPTER EIGHTEEN

S kol stood before his master and bowed his head.
He'd be damned if he knelt like Blas had the
moment he spied Alshan Ra. Ra's disciples milled about,
preparing their devices and concealing them with their
robes. Skol felt a prick of uncertainty as he stood among a
room filled with explosives, but he knew that, of all the
things Alshan Ra might be, he was not suicidal.

If Skol was to die, it would not be because Alshan Ra
ordered the detonation of the explosives there. No, were
he to die, Skol had no doubt Alshan Ra would go about it
in a different, more personal manner.

"You wished to speak to me, Master?" Skol asked as his
master's eyes roamed around the room, taking in his
acolytes. Skol saw the glee plainly there. People would die
today, many of them, and Alshan Ra was going to revel in
their demise and give praise to Elerus for the bloodshed.

Alshan Ra turned his gaze on Skol. "I did indeed." He
raised a finger to belay any further comments, and the

master turned to Blas. "Suit up and make ready to meet Elerus," he told the man.

The disciple raised his head and stared wide-eyed at Alshan Ra, and Skol almost laughed at his shocked expression.

"Join your brothers," Alshan Ra told him, being clearer this time so there was no misunderstanding. "Join the war. Suit up."

Blas staggered to his feet and visibly swallowed hard. Alshan Ra grinned at him and waved another of his acolytes over.

"Prepare him."

The disciple nodded and practically dragged Blas away, over to where the rest of the zealots were strapping on bombs. Skol followed him until he disappeared into the swarming crowd, then he turned back to Alshan Ra.

The man stared back at him without blinking.

"I hope you don't expect me to strap on a bomb and go gleefully into the hereafter, Master," Skol said, letting the sliver of a smirk play across his lips.

Alshan Ra grinned at his impudence. "I've no such task set for you, Skol Arduin." He shook his head. "No, no menial self-sacrifice for you," he whispered low enough that only Skol heard him.

"Then why is it you asked to see me?"

"I brought you here to witness your failure," Alshan Ra told him.

Skol sighed, realizing his earlier presumption was correct. Alshan Ra had brought him here to teach him the error of his ways, and Skol regretted allowing his men to remain outside.

On the other hand, he hoped Vetrus enjoyed being in charge, however long it lasted.

Alshan Ra brought up a holo on the screen mounted nearby, and Skol recognized the arena, though he had no understanding as to why the man would show him that.

"What is this?" he asked, then he spotted the dark-outfitted warriors battling the automaton and recognized them as the Furlorians from their battle with his droids. "Ah, I see."

Skol moved closer to the screen to better see the battle play out. "May I ask how is this a failure if the fools were made to fight the automaton? Warpath surely made short work of these operatives, whether they ever truly worked for the Etheric Federation or not."

"Continue to watch," Alshan Ra prompted, and Skol felt a knot tighten in his stomach. While his master was fond of theatrics, especially in front of the disciples, he rarely ever displayed that side to Skol.

That told him he was about to witness something he didn't want to.

And sure enough, a moment later, the screens brightened to the point of searing his eyes. When it normalized, Skol saw the fallout of the flare. He stared at the screen in disbelief as one of the black-clad Furlorians stood in the hand of the automaton, pistol leveled, and the giant metal beast with its face turned into a searing crater.

Skol sighed, chin dropping to his chest.

If he had nothing else, he still had his honor.

He turned away from his master and looked out at the crowd of zealots who stood stock still and stared at him.

"Have them do it then," Skol told Alshan Ra, meeting the eyes of the disciples until they looked away.

Alshan Ra came over and stood alongside him, waving at his acolytes. "I would never let such filth dishonor your memory, Skol Arduin." Smiling and motioning them on, he told the robed men, "Go and make Elerus proud."

The acolytes followed his order without question and filled out of the building until there were only a handful left. Skol watched as Blas shuffled toward the door, doing his best to be last to avoid being part of what was soon to happen.

He stared at Skol, who simply smiled back and offered a farewell nod as the last of the acolytes helped usher him out and closed the door behind them.

Maybe I am more than Blas after all, Skol thought.

And that was the last thing he *ever* thought as Alshan Ra drove a blade through the base of his neck and up into his skull.

"May Elerus welcome you to her breast with open arms, child," Alshan Ra said as Skol's world sank toward eternal darkness. "Destiny awaits."

CHAPTER NINETEEN

After dropping Grom off in his hideout, Taj and Dent raced to meet Lina and the rest of the crew near the palatial gardens. They realized a few short minutes later just how daunting a task Taj had set for them when they caught up to them in a narrow alley off the main track.

"About time," Torbon sniped as Taj and Dent ran up alongside the crew. A crush of people milled about cheerfully on the street just a short distance away on the other side of them.

"Where's the courtyard?" Taj asked.

"This is it," Lina replied. "Well, that is actually," she clarified, pointing beyond a short wall of barriers at the end of the alley and at the backs of the thousands of people clustered together. "The stage is on the far side of all this, by the way." Lina looped her hand around to kind of give an example of the location.

Taj swallowed hard as she stared out over the heads of the crowd, the courtyard at the slightest of declines to allow for each successive row of people to get an equally clear view. And just like Dent had said, there had to be thousands of people there, all crammed in together. It was the perfect environment for a massacre.

She watched as they waved banners and cheered, smiles apparently the outfit of the day among the serpentine crowd.

"What the gack do they have to be so happy about?" she asked.

"Not much, really." Dent shook his head.

"Then why are they smiling like that?" She jabbed a finger at the crowd.

"This regime is quite totalitarian in its rule," the AI explained. "It's either join the crowd and smile and celebrate like everyone else or have the Heltrol visit you in the middle of the night. You can imagine how that might turn out."

Taj groaned. She really wished then that she'd spent more time researching the mission and the people she'd be dealing with. Maybe that was part of what General Reynolds wanted out of her and the crew, for them to understand the true complexity of what it was they were asking for when they asked to join the Federation.

Taj sighed as she imagined the General thinking exactly that as he sent the crew into space on their very first *mission*.

If that were the case, she'd need to watch the man more carefully next time he sent them off as it was clear he was far more devious than his direct, friendly nature let on.

Taj shook those thoughts away. She needed to be focused on the here and now.

"Were you able to stop any of the zealots?" she asked.

Lina shook her head. "The crowd was here already," she replied. "By the time we showed up, the zealots were moving into the audience. It was too late."

Taj looked at her friend and noticed the paleness around her normally-bright eyes. She felt instantly bad for her, knowing Lina was taking all this personal. When people died out in the crowd today, Lina would be thinking it was her fault, no matter how untrue that was.

Taj realized she'd be thinking the same way soon enough.

"We need to get up to the stage where we can warn the queen," Taj said, looking around for a way to do just that.

"Unlikely," Dent told her. He gestured toward the barricades. "Look closer."

She did and spotted a number of battle droids set along the edge of the throng where she hadn't noticed them earlier.

On top of that, there were a number of Heltrol soldiers patrolling both within the crowd and around it, and the crew had to turn away a couple times to avoid being identified as they marched past.

Taj looked around more and spotted what looked like an army of Heltrol snipers on the roofs, as well.

"They're going all out," Taj stated, impressed by the queen's defenses despite her security services ignoring Dent's anonymous warnings and his inability to get in touch with Zel.

She thought for a moment that maybe the queen would be safe enough given the massive array of multi-tiered security amassed in the area.

Maybe she and the crew could step back and let the Heltrol handle it. The queen's safety wasn't what they were there for, after all. While Taj would no doubt regret the loss of life that happened, could she truly be blamed for it?

And while the answer was no, Taj knew there was no way she could allow anything to happen without trying her best to stop it.

That simply wasn't who she was.

Besides, she knew the leader of the Heltrol couldn't be trusted.

Still, she wasn't sure what she *could* do.

This far away from the stage, there was simply no way to get a message to the queen without drawing undue attention to themselves. And between the zealots and the Heltrol gunning for them, she couldn't see how any of them would manage to get close enough to make a difference.

Taj moved right up to the barricades, coughing and looking away as a Heltrol soldier slid through the crowd just a couple meters away. Once the soldier was gone, she eased onto the barricade itself, staying low enough not to draw attention to herself.

From her position, she had a clear view of the stage, though it looked as if ants crawled across it, she was so far away. She adjusted her eyepiece and zoomed in, immediately wishing she hadn't.

There, a short distance behind the array of microphones where Taj knew Queen Rilan would be speaking to her people, stood Commander Rolkar and the thin, pale Zel.

Armed and armored as always, Rolkar stood at attention, looking the perfect little soldier in her black and red outfit. Her weapon was within easy grasp and from the looks of it, only poor old Zel was anywhere near enough to stop her should she do something horrible.

Taj cursed, and Cabe came up behind her, setting a hand on her side.

"What?"

Taj dropped down to face him and the rest of the crew that joined them.

"Commander Rolkar's on the stage," she stated, snarling. "There are soldiers at her back, but there's no one but Zel between her and the queen once she's on stage."

Krawg glanced over at Dent. "Ship guns?"

Dent gave an apologetic shake of his head. "The automaton was made of sufficiently dense enough material that it absorbed the brunt of the *Arrant*'s weakest blast and there was little concern about the shot traveling through the thing."

He motioned toward the crowd and stage.

"If I unleash that kind of firepower here, we might as well walk away and let the zealots kill who they will. It would end up being far less than we would in our attempt to save people."

"Yeah, let's not up the body count," Cabe agreed. "I think there's been more than enough already."

"I agree," Taj said. "Which means we're gonna need to do something soon, even if it's something stupid and reckless."

"So, the same as most every other plan?" Krawg asked for confirmation.

Taj thought about it for a second and nodded. "Yeah, pretty much, it looks like."

The crowd erupted into a frenzy, and Taj knew exactly what that meant. The queen had arrived.

Taj spun around and clambered back onto the barrier, zooming in on the stage. Sure enough, the queen was regally waltzing onto the stage, having just passed the legion of soldiers who would be guarding her back.

She stepped by Rolkar and Zel and offered both a smile on her way toward the microphones. Taj felt sick seeing the woman be so friendly to Rolkar.

Then she reached the microphone array and greeted the crowd to massive applause. The queen droned on in the background, thanking her people for their turnout, which Taj scoffed at having realized it was forced, and went on about how long it had been since she'd seen her sibling and how happy she was to have him returned to the kingdom and the planet.

Taj listened to the woman prattle on, knowing how short time was, and she wished she could scream loud enough to be heard all the way to the stage.

And then an idea hit her.

"Dent! Lina!" she called out.

The pair came closer, and Taj glanced over her shoulder at them without relinquishing her spot on the barrier.

"Can either of you take control of the PA system?"

Lina's eyes brightened. "Oh Rowl, that is genius."

"Hmmm," Dent muttered. "I wonder why I didn't think of that."

Taj tapped the side of her head. "Logic?"

"You're getting there." Dent nodded before turning to

face Lina, the pair hunkering down over the screens on their arms. "Let's see if we can isolate the frequency."

"It'll be tough since I can't imagine this is the first time someone's tried it on them before."

"No doubt, but no one on this planet has our acumen, do they?"

"Gacking straight they don't," Lina shouted, her fingers flying over her keypad.

Taj took a deep breath and looked away from the confusing mess of numbers and symbols the two were working on, looking back to the stage. Another roar went up as she did.

Her heart skipped a beat when she saw who had joined the queen on stage.

The man strode up to the microphones to a roaring celebration that rivaled anything Taj had heard in the arena. Yet Taj couldn't make a sound. Her throat seized and threatened to close on her, choking her breath away.

It wasn't until Queen Rolkar kissed the man on the cheek and turned to the crowd, announcing him, that Taj broke free of the spell she'd fallen under.

"May I introduce, once again, my dearest brother, Alshan Ra, Prince Regent of Zoranthan," she said. "Welcome him home."

The crowd erupted, and Taj slipped from her perch.

"Oh...gack," she managed to spit out.

The crew, clearly seeing her reaction, moved into position to get a better look, and they all froze, staring wide-eyed at the stage where the leader of the zealots stood hand-in-hand with the queen.

Brother, Taj thought, the word springing to mind as she gawked at the stage. And then it all made sense.

"Oh, no, no, no," she cried out, realization striking hard. "Dent! Grom didn't mean *his* brother, he meant the queen's! He was warning us!"

Those words barely out of her mouth when a dozen explosions erupted in the crowd, filling the air with screams of terror and cruel black smoke.

CHAPTER TWENTY

Explosion after explosion rang out, and Taj's heart ached with every one of them.

The zealots had begun their work, and innocents were paying the price for it.

The crowd, dying in fiery agony, surged and pushed outward, desperately trying to flee the carnage.

Without reason to hold back any longer, Taj leapt over the barriers and into the crowd, pushing hard toward the stage with everything she had. She knew without looking back that the crew was doing the same.

"Clear the crowd," she screamed over the comm and pushed on. "Save as many as you can!"

Another explosion erupted nearby, and Taj felt nameless debris patter off her armor. She did her best not to imagine it for what it truly was.

Instead, she pressed harder, shoving people out of her way and leaping over their heads to clear as much distance as possible with every spurt of motion.

She noticed the crowd had peeled away from the stage, fleeing and scattering in every direction to get away, but the Heltrol held their ground, pushing them back into the conflagration.

Taj realized then that the zealots had known that would happen, had been counting on it. Bile rose in the back of her throat, but Taj denied it, swallowing it back. She would not let these murderers, these butchers, win.

She leapt over the crowd again, aiming her sights on the stage while she had a few seconds of unobstructed view.

Queen Rilan stood at the microphones, staring out at the crowd with wide, wet eyes. Taj could see fear in her rigid posture, in the stiffness of her jaw, her mouth cracked open in disbelief.

The zealot leader had eased back, leaving his sister to her astonishment. There was no hint of concern or caring in his expression. He looked only as if he wanted to retreat from the chaos and slip away.

Taj landed and leapt again, apologizing in her mind to the people she bowled over as she loped through the throng, trying to reach the queen.

While she was in the air again, she caught sight of Commander Rolkar. The woman had her pistol out and was racing forward, straight toward Queen Rilan, who still stood there frozen in shock.

Zel, to Taj's amazement, had launched himself at the queen even quicker than Rolkar had. He streaked across the stage, his robes fluttering behind him as though he was flying.

Taj was impressed by his tenacity as he raced to protect

his queen despite being an old, infirm man with a questionable sense of reality.

Taj pictured his confusion in the vehicle after they'd been ambushed. He'd been terrified, and Rolkar had to comfort him to keep him calm.

Fury warmed Taj's cheeks as she pictured Rolkar sitting so close, plotting, planning, waiting for this moment. And here it was, and the only person who could stop the queen from dying was pathetic old Zel.

Commander Rolkar raised her pistol and took aim, and Taj shrieked at the top of her lungs.

Zealots reached the last line of the Heltrol and detonated their bombs, blowing away the last defense between the queen and the zealots in the crowd. But Taj knew she had a greater worry right then: the assassin at her back.

Taj hit the ground once more and threw everything into the last leap she knew she'd get before all hope was lost.

She soared above what remained of the crowd, charred bodies and billows of smoke, but Taj refused to look down, to acknowledge what was there. She'd have to face it soon enough, but not now.

No, now she needed to save the queen.

Taj willed her weapon to her hand and raised it in front of her, struggling to target Rolkar as she flew through the air like an errant missile.

Her eyepiece zoned in, and Taj could see the desperation and the sheer determination on Commander Rolkar's face as she lowered her weapon and made ready to fire while the scene around the queen turned into a blur.

Steel glinted under the bright lights.

Taj saw deep into Rolkar's eyes. There was pain there, fury, and something else Taj didn't immediately recognize.

And then she did and felt even sicker than before.

She squeezed the trigger.

CHAPTER TWENTY-ONE

Taj's shot was perfect.

Commander Rolkar froze as Zel Ga'Vor, the queen's representative, gaped at the sudden hole blown through his chest. The man stumbled as the queen spun about, watching him as he fell face-first to the ground, wisps of smoke billowing out from beneath him.

The knife he'd raised clattered to the stage and slid to a stop at the queen's feet. Her gaze was torn between it and her man, gasping his last in front of her.

As Taj landed, Commander Rolkar tossed her gun aside as she reached the queen, wrapping her arms around the woman in a protective embrace that spoke of more than simple loyalty.

She loved her queen, that much was clear.

And Taj had nearly killed Rolkar, so focused as she was on her dislike of the woman and her mistakes.

Had Taj not spied the knife slip loose of Zel's robed sleeve, had she not realized that the man who'd cowered in the caravan vehicle shouldn't be able to move so quickly or so gracefully across the stage, Taj might well have killed the wrong person.

But she hadn't, and Taj could finally breathe again, guilt and anguish giving way to relief.

She ran toward the stage, the way now clear, soldiers and citizens dead all around, but despite the shot that had saved the queen's life, it hadn't been enough.

Alshan Ra stepped up behind the queen and Rolkar and drove a blade into the commander's back.

Rolkar shrieked and went to lash out, but Alshan Ra struck her with the knife again, then again, ripping the commander loose of his sister and hurling the soldier aside. She stumbled to the stage, hands still grasping to protect her queen.

Then Alshan Ra's forearm wrapped around his sister's throat, the blade leveled to her eye just as Taj leapt onto the stage.

"Stay back, Furlorian," Alshan Ra warned, nicking his sister's cheek and drawing a drop of blood. "I *will* kill her."

Taj dropped her gun and raised her hands to pacify him. "I believe you. Don't."

The zealot master glared at her, and she could see the absolute hatred boiling within his four eyes.

"You will not take this moment from me, Federation lackey."

Taj said nothing, only inching forward as best she could without him realizing it.

Can anyone shoot him? she asked across the mental link.

No clear shot, Dent's thoughts came back immediately. *Queen's in the way. I'm repositioning.*

Hurry, she told him. *Running out of time here.*

"This throne should be mine!" Alshan Ra screamed. "She stole this from me. It was my destiny, my inheritance as foretold by the great goddess Elerus. She promised me this!"

Froth flew from his mouth as he raged, and Taj feared for the queen's life. The blade pressed harder against her cheek, where a rivulet of blood ran down her face and dripped from her chin.

"Don't hurt her," Taj begged, still trying to close the distance between them, trying to buy time for Dent to get a clear shot. Something.

Anything.

"Don't hurt her?" Alshan Ra shrieked at Taj, nearly howling, his voice was so forceful. "Don't hurt her?"

He backed toward the side of the stage, seeking a way out. Taj spied the wreckage of the Heltrol who'd been stationed at the back, and saw the remnants of the zealots that had decimated them at some point during the chaos.

Alshan Ra pressed the blade deeper, drawing more blood from Queen Rilan. She cried out, his grip tightening at her throat, and that was when Taj saw just how much her brother really did want to hurt her.

That was all he wanted to do.

And if Taj or the others didn't stop him, and he couldn't use the queen as a shield to get away, that was exactly what he *would* do.

She was alive only because he needed her alive if there was any hope of him escaping with his life. She was all that stood between his getting away or not, and his self-preservation was the only thing that kept her alive.

Come on, Dent, where are you? Taj asked over the link

There was no reply.

Taj needed to act.

She willed all the power she could into her suit and went to pounce. She could close the distance quickly enough. She'd done it in practice. She knew she could do it.

Only no one's lives had been at stake in practice.

Still…

"Don't you do it!" Alshan Ra yelled, waving his blade her direction as he recognized Taj stiffening up, readying to act.

Then Alshan Ra's eyes went wide.

He stumbled, and Queen Rilan broke free as his arm lost its strength. She lurched forward and fell, crashing onto the stage and crawling away from her brother.

Alshan Ra dropped to his knees, and standing behind him, however unbelievably, stood Grom Hadar. The knife he'd used to stab the zealot master remained in the man's back where he'd driven it deep.

Alshan Ra turned slowly toward Grom, his own knife still in his hands. Too weak to do much of anything, Grom toppled to the floor in front of the queen's murderous brother. He laid still, staring at Alshan Ra with resignation, but there was something else there, too.

Satisfaction.

He'd saved the queen.

He was okay losing his life doing that.

Commander Rolkar, however, had something else in mind.

At some point during the scuffle, she'd crawled across the stage and reclaimed her pistol.

Eyes hazy and filled with agony, she shot Alshan Ra dead before he could bring his knife to bear on Grom.

Taj let out a shuddering breath as she watched Alshan Ra collapse, and then her sight was blocked by a horde of Heltrol soldiers storming the stage. They formed a wall and pushed Taj back as they collected their queen and commander and rushed the pair away to safety.

Once they were gone, Taj went over to Grom and dropped down beside him, helping him to sit upright. The man grunted and stared out at the crowd where her crew continued to aid the people who needed it as best as they could.

Taj watched them with pride as she gathered the strength to go help them.

"You ready to go home, Grom?" she asked.

Grom Hadar managed a nod and the barest sliver of a smile.

"R-ready."

EPILOGUE

In the throne room days after the massacre, Taj stared up at Queen Rilan as she sat on the throne, set upon the dais. Her face had been patched up, though she'd barely had a scratch and it looked fine.

Commander Rolkar was absent, her injuries too grievous to easily repair and get her up and about. Taj had heard she would survive and would have no lasting ill effects, except for some impressive scars. And despite all of Taj's earlier misgivings about the woman, she was glad she would be okay.

The zealots, what was left of them, had been rounded up and sentenced to death by the crown, and Taj thought that was a pretty fitting end, all things considered.

Her crew gathered around her. Cabe had his hand in a splint, but the rest were hale and whole, for which Taj was grateful. They'd seen enough the last few days to haunt them for a long time, and Taj was glad none of those scars would be more serious than a few nights of lost sleep.

"So, is it true you do not really have access to the Toradium-42 you initially offered?" Queen Rilan asked.

Taj smiled. "I'm sorry, but we don't. We lost our planet months ago and might never get to return. The mineral resides there, a foul alien army tearing apart our home to steal it away."

The queen sighed. "That's too bad. But if you ever do find your way back there and reclaim your planet, please, keep the Orgesse in mind."

Taj bowed and offered the queen a conciliatory nod.

Not on your gacking life, she thought, grinning ferally as they said their good-byes and returned to the *Arrant,* where Grom Hadar waited to be taken to the Federation.

Back on the space station *Corzant,* Taj and her crew sat in the meeting room where Lance Reynolds had first offered them the mission of rescuing Grom Hadar.

A lot had changed since then, mostly Taj.

As she waited for the General to make his appearance via view screen, she looked around the table at the people who mattered the most to her.

They'd proven themselves during the mission, and she couldn't have been prouder at how they'd handled themselves. Thousands of lives on Zoranthan had been saved because of their efforts, and she only hoped they knew how much she truly appreciated them.

She'd make sure they did.

The crew sat there quietly until the screens flickered, glad for the silence for once, and General Reynolds appeared. Unlike before, he looked rested and back to his robust self.

"I've read your reports," he said, foregoing any casual greeting. "Very impressive. You've acquitted yourself with honor and grace. The Federation thanks you."

He looked out over the crew, their situations reversed— the Furlorians and their friends the ones tired and frayed and in need of a vacation.

"We owe you a debt of gratitude," the General said. "We have already promised you a planet, a new home where you can all begin again, both the Furlorians and the Dandrinites, and we'll make good on that promise as soon as humanly possible."

The General smiled at their reactions to the news, pausing for just a moment before going on.

"That said, if there is anything else we can offer you to show our appreciation, please don't hesitate to ask."

"General." Taj raised her hand. "If I might."

"Please," he replied. "That wasn't just lip service. You want it, ask."

Taj glanced around the table at her companions, taking a second to examine each, before she turned back to the view screen.

"I'd like to take you up on that offer, sir," she told him, rising to her feet to look him in the eyes as best she could.

"Name it," he said.

"We could use an army," she requested. "We'd like to go home."

Howdy folks!

Here we are on the third book of Enemy of My Enemy, and I hope you're enjoying reading about these misfit cats as much as I'm enjoying writing about them. Getting a chance to write in the Kurtherian Gambit world with both these books and working with Craig Martelle in the new Superdreadnought series has been amazing, and I'm loving all the feedback we're getting in reviews and online, so keep it up please. Every bit of it is awesome.

I'm working on book four of Enemy of My Enemy right now, as well as Superdreadnought 2, and I can't wait to get these books out to you. Enemy four will end the current arc of stories for the Furlorians, but it most certainly won't be the last you see of them. New stories and ideas are in the works, and I can't wait to share them with you.

This whole process has been a fantastic experience, and we couldn't do it without you. So, raise a beer (or your drink of choice) to yourself and shout cheers real loud because you deserve it.

Thank you so much for reading and hanging out with us. You folks rock. See you soon with more words.

Tim Marquitz

AUTHOR NOTES - MICHAEL ANDERLE

WRITTEN OCTOBER 21, 2018

Author Notes (on behalf of Michael Anderle):

Thank you for reading! Once again, all the way to the end and beyond! I'm glad you liked this latest iteration of Enemy of My Enemy. Michael is not a cat guy, but he wants to be. He wants to retire to Cabo San Lucas where he can surround himself with the world's greatest hunters. Maybe not, but he's not opposed to cats, as long as they aren't climbing on him, unless they are.

When Tim talked about the plot for this one, we wanted to focus on the main characters, without distraction in a way that you could get a better feel for Taj and her leadership skills as well as how the supporting cast could measure up. Are they a strike team for the Federation or a bunch of cats trying to get home?

How about both?

When I first read the story, I was as happy as could be about the plot and character development. Well done to Tim Marquitz for another out of this world winner!

I'm not in the sub-arctic right now, but in Illinois spending time with my brother after the passing of his wife a little over a week ago. His wife was in pain for a long time. It is comforting to know that she doesn't have to suffer any longer. It's also sad that her newest grandson was born after her stroke but before she passed. His birthday is one day prior to the day of her death. We will all miss her. We welcome the family's greatest sleeper – this little guy, Junior, is an all-star when it comes to rack time.

Part of returning to normal for my brother is wargaming, so that's where we're at – a gaming convention playing fantasy role-playing games. We went after the town bad guy in a marathon session yesterday. Today, we'll have some new challenge awaiting our stalwart characters. I ate a Wisconsin bratwurst that wanted to carry on a conversation well into the night, but through perseverance, I held him at bay.

Traveling like this, I've discovered that I like the Starbucks iced coffee mochas that you can buy everywhere. I've probably had more of them than I should have, but we'll chalk it up to stress coffee drinking

I look forward to getting home to sleep in my own bed. Slept in four different places over the past week – a chair, a couch, and three separate beds.

And tomorrow (publication day) is my birthday! I'll be traveling all day on my way back home to Alaska. I hope I'm able to access the net and get my newsletter out to announce both these releases. I'm a big fan of our fans. I appreciate anyone who takes the time to read one of our stories and then comes back for the next ones. You are the real heroes of these stories. Our intent is to take you away from the real world, for a little while, leaving you happy at the end because the good guys have won. You know there's more for them to do, but for now, you're satisfied that they were able to come through.

With that, it's time to go. I have morning stuff to do before heading to the game show to play a morning session before driving back to my brother's house to wrap up the week and get ready for my flight tomorrow morning.

Go forth and do great things. If you're thinking about someone, drop them a line, give a call, send a card. You'll never know if you won't get another chance.

Peace, fellow humans

Craig

BOOKS BY TIM MARQUITZ

Also Available from Tim Marquitz

The Demon Squad Series

From Hell (Novella)
DS1 - Armageddon Bound
DS2 - Resurrection
Betrayal (Intro short to At the Gates)
DS3 - At the Gates
DS4 - Echoes of the Past
DS5 - Beyond the Veil
DS6 - The Best of Enemies
DS7 - Exit Wounds
DS8 - Collateral Damage
DS9 – Aftermath
DS10 – Institutionalized
To Hell and Back - A Demon Squad Collection (books 1-3)

The Blood War Trilogy

Dawn of War
Embers of an Age
Requiem

Clandestine Daze Series

Eyes Deep (novella)
Influx

Standalone Fantasy

Dirge
Witch Bane
War God Rising

Sci-fi

Excalibur

Dead West

Those Poor, Poor Bastards
The Ten Thousand Things
Omnibus 1

Horror

Prey
Serial

Skulls
Heir to the Blood Throne: Inheritance

Collections

Tales of Magic and Misery

Non-Fiction

Memoirs of a Machine – w/John MACHINE Lober
Grunt Style: The Blue Collar Guide to Writing Genre
Fiction

Anthologies

Blackguards (Ragnarok Publications)
Unbound (Grim Oak Press)
SNAFU: Survival of the Fittest (Cohesion Press)
SNAFU: Hunters (Cohesion Press)
SNAFU: Future Warfare (Cohesion Press)
SNAFU: Black Ops (Cohesion Press)
In the Shadow of the Towers (Night Shade)
Neverland's Library (Ragnarok Publications)
At Hell's Gates 1&3 (Charity)
American Nightmare (Kraken Press)
Corrupts Absolutely? (Ragnarok Publications)
Widowmakers (Charity)
That Hoodoo Voodoo, That You Do (Ragnarok
Publications)

BOOKS BY MICHAEL ANDERLE

For a complete list of books by Michael Anderle, please visit:

www.lmbpn.com/ma-books/

All LMBPN Audiobooks are Available at Audible.com and iTunes

To see all LMBPN audiobooks, including those written by
Michael Anderle please visit:

www.lmbpn.com/audible